THE
GOLDEN MARRIAGE

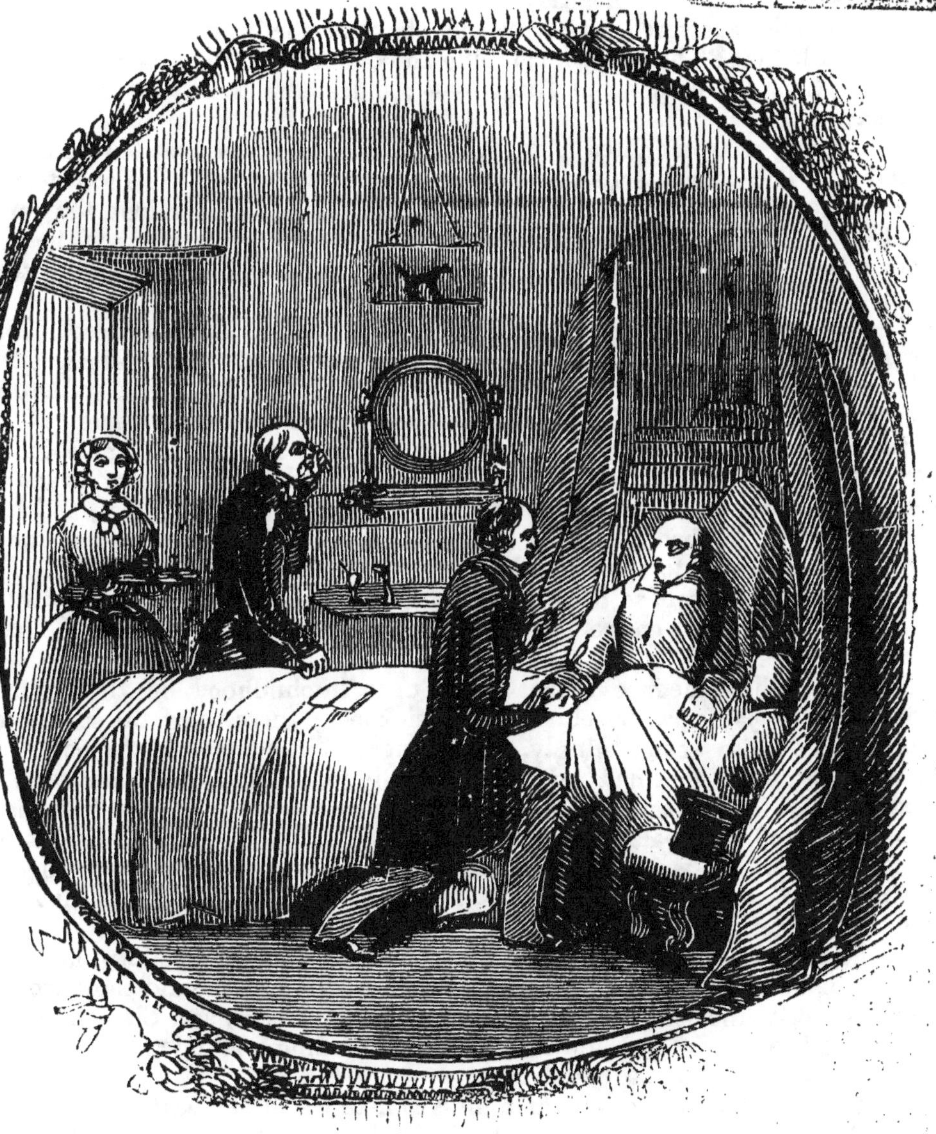

CHAPTER I.

THE PROMISE.

"Keep silence, daughter of Frivolity, for Death is in that chamber!
  Startle not with echoing sound the strangely-solemn place.
  Death is here in spirit!"

THE sun was going down in the west, in the autumn of 18—, when an eastern stage-coach drew up at the door of a country mansion, old and venerable in appearance. A young man leaped out, waved his hand in silent farewell to his fellow-travellers, and, leaving his baggage to the care of a servant, entered the house

No. 1

In the hall he was met by an old grey-haired man, who, hearing the coach stop, had hastened to meet his young master.

The young man looked inquiringly into the face of the man, as if expecting the answer to a question he almost feared to ask; and what he read there only strengthened his worst fears.

"How is he, James?" he asked.

The old man answered with a solemn shake of the head.

"He still lives?" he gasped, catching the old servant by the arm.

"Yes, he still breathes, but I fear ——; indeed he is very ill, sir. I am glad you have come."

The young man mounted a flight of well-worn stairs that led to his father's chamber. The door was ajar, and the stillness that reigned within made his heart ache. Trembling, he leaned a few moments for support against the jamb, too much overcome to proceed; but, hearing old James's soft tread upon the stairs, he made a last effort, swallowed down the deep risings in his throat, and entered the room.

There is something in a sick room that always strikes us with dread. The windows darkened to a shadow; different coloured phials and glasses, sitting in cabalistic mystery around; the air, perfumed almost to faintness, steals upon the senses like a spell, and strikes a damp to the very centre of our being.

Such was the room entered by our hero. It had one redeeming feature, however; a few bright rays from the setting sun found their way in, aslant the old elms in the yard, and through a rent in the hangings of the window, and fell their full blaze upon the bed where lay the dying man—a mediator between the mortal and immortal—as if to cheer and light his soul's pathway back to its God.

The young man stole to the bed, and stood in silent grief over the still form of his father. A great change had come over him in the three years he had been absent from his home.

There was the same face he had looked upon in childhood, but the features were sharpened and pale now, by old age and sickness; there were the same eyes that had looked on him encouragingly, when engaged in some athletic boyish sport; there the same lips that had given him kindly counsel—silent now, and still as chiselled marble; the same hand that had rested upon his head in blessing, when last they parted, now palsied lay, and the blue veins looked out through the thin transparency of the wrinkled skin. He was the same, yet, oh, how changed! It was more striking to the son, perhaps, for he had left him in health, and returned to find him wan and emaciated to the very grave.

As he bent over him, his heart almost bursting with his feelings, he placed his hand in his father's. The dying man's lips moved, but no sound came from them; his eyes slowly unclosed, and became fixed upon his son, and the gentle pressure of the hand he felt, robbed him of his little remaining fortitude, and, sinking upon his knees, he sobbed like a child.

Do not think him weak—'tis manliness sometimes to be heart-broken. Imagine yourself, dear reader, standing by the bed-side of your only surviving parent—a father—whose whole life had been marked by his peculiar regard and affection, every year bringing with it some new token of his love—each day of the year some fresh remembrance of his untiring devotion to your wants and happiness, and then, when all you possess speaks of this dear friend—when everything around breathes of his presence—when everything you love is associated with him—every thought, every wish from childhood centred in him—then to see him on the bed of sickness; to see him leaving you, the last and best of earthly friends, to the sympathies of a selfish world—alone! Have you now no tears?

The dying man's mouth being wet by the nurse standing at his head, he was able faintly to articulate, "Philip!"

"Father!" sobbed the son.

"God has heard my prayers, and sent thee in time for a father's last blessing. I am glad of it, for I have something to say to thee, my boy, very near my heart."

"Speak— speak,"

"Helen—your marriage."

"Do not speak of that, father; waste not strength with thoughts of me, I beseech you."

"How can I better employ it than for your happiness, my son? Nay, I must speak now, for I feel I shall not be here long. You know I am set upon this marriage, Philip; I promised her father, on *his* death-bed, to use my influence to bring it about. He was a dear friend of mine, as you know; our intimacy commenced long before we went to college, and when there, we were chums. He was a sterling fellow, an honourable man, and I was proud to wear him in my heart."

"Cease, father; some other time."

"After years," continued the dying man, with some difficulty, "brought with it nothing to interrupt the perfect harmony of our feelings, and we settled down in life like brothers in one family. On his death-bed, my friend (his wife being dead, and your mother having gone to her long home) spoke of the friendship that had existed between us from boyhood, and requested that it might be kept up by the union of our children. My friend spoke of it with tears in his eyes, and I promised to use my best endeavours to bring it about. That was five years ago— before you went to college."

The dying man ceased, for his strength was fast failing; and it was with the greatest difficulty he had spoken thus far. He seemed to wait his son's reply.

"I know but little of her, father; I have not seen her for years—since she went to reside with her brother, in the city."

"Neither have I, my son; but I have made repeated inquiries of her, and though I hear by some that she is a little gay, I doubt not she has her father's good heart, and will make you an affectionate wife. He was a wild dog, when a boy, but a true friend."

"What would you have me do, father?" asked Philip, willing to do any thing to relieve him from the conversation that he saw was too much for his little remaining strength. "Speak, I am ready to obey."

"Bless thee, my boy! You were always a dutiful son, and ready to obey my slightest wish. It is a comfort to me now."

Here the dying man paused, and his pale lips trembled with the intensity of his feelings.

"I would have thee wed thy little playmate, Helen Freelove, my son. Do not receive this as a command, but as a dear wish of my heart; as it was the last wish of my friend."

"It shall be as you wish, dear father, if she but consent to it. Calm yourself now, and try and get some rest."

"There is no more rest for me, my son, until I taste the rest of the grave,—the sleep that is never broken. I feel it is close at hand. I have felt its cold hand upon me for hours; but the good angel heard my prayers, and let me live to see thee once more. Thank God for it."

"Dear, dear father!"

For a minute the dying man was silent, as if taking leave of every earthly thing in thought, and then said, fervently,

"Father! my work is finished; I wait thy good pleasure."

Sinking down, a smile played over his thin features, like that of a child confidently resting in the arms of its parent; while Philip, still holding him by the hand, buried his face in the bed clothes.

The doctor, meantime, had arrived, and entered the room. He saw, at once, by the charge that had taken place in his patient, that he was dying, and stood behind Philip with arms folded, coldly looking on; for he had witnessed many a death-bed scene, and like Griffon, philosophised on every case he was brought to witness.

Old James and the nurse stood at the foot of the bed, their tears attesting their grief which was silent and respectful.

Thus the solemn stillness of the room was only broken by the deep grief of Philip while without Nature was one unceasing anthem. The sun had gone down, and the gentle breeze just stirred the branches of the trees, and flapped the window curtains back and forth, bringing in the odours of sweet flowers, and the song of the night birds ; and adding, too, the chirping of the crickets and the deep bass of the bullfrog ; all harmonising, and lulling the dying into his last repose.

Philip held his father's hand, till its coldness startled him, and told the tale. He was fatherless !

CHAPTER II.

THE JOURNEY.

> " Life is a strange avenue of various trees and flowers ;
> Lightsome at commencement, but darkening to its end
> in a distant massy portal."

PHILIP ERWIN, at the time we commence our story, was twenty-two years of age Few young men possessed better advantages, or were reared with a gentler hand. He lost his mother when a mere boy, but her place was supplied by a faithful nurse, not less kind than that mother would have been, had she been spared to him.

His father had been a practical farmer. Possessed of immense means, he scrupled not to use it lavishly where any thing connected with his favourite pursuit (agriculture) was concerned. He had been a warm friend and father. It is not impossible but he showed more regard for his son, that he watched him with more tender care, than he would have done had his mother been spared to him, the guide so necessary to the wants of childhood, and that the paternal tie was strengthened by the breaking of all other ties. Thus he had been a friend and associate as well as father.

Six months had gone by, and early summer, with its flowers, had come again. The barbed arrow of grief had lost its poignancy, and Philip began to look about him, remembering he had duties to perform towards the living as well as to the dead.

Not that he thought of a wife, but as the last wish of his father ; but having made the promise, he would see Helen—she to whom, with her consent, he was to be united, and judge if in the union he should be happy or miserable.

He had not seen her for years ; he could form no idea of her looks, as a young lady ; but his recollections of the child were pleasing. He knew but little of women, as his father had always lived in seclusion, and when at college, he seldom joined in the gay parties with his fellow students ; yet he had formed some ideas, (whether true or false, is not for us to say) of the requisite qualities in a young lady necessary for his happiness.

A few evenings subsequent to forming this determination, found Philip—after receiving a long cautionary lecture from his faithful nurse, to guard him against the dangers and temptations of the town, and a fervent " God bless you" from old James—in a stage coach, bound eastward.

It was before the days of the " iron horse," when railways were scarcely known, certainly never dreamed of, over " wild mountainous Vermont ;" and a journey from S——ville to Boston was of as much importance as one from Boston to Niagara Falls, in these days of steam and Yankee go-a-head-ative-ness. Now the distance is travelled between sun and sun ; then it was a journey of eight and forty hours.

The mountain stage was little crowded on this morning, but as it proceeded " down country," as it is termed, its vacant seats, one by one, were occupied. On the morning of the second day, when Erwin went to take his seat in the coach, the middle seat, which he had monopolised on the previous day, was taken up by a young lady ; and as there was no vacant seat inside, he was forced to take up with the accommodations of the driver, who had already two gentlemen on the seat behind him.

On mounting the box, Erwin took a good look at his neighbours for the day. The one seated nearest him was evidently of that class denominated "Yankees." His large, full, round face bore the mingled expression of good sense and its opposite. At first, you would see but a silly beaming and lurking drollery in every expression ; but on scanning his face closely, you would discover good sense crouching in the back ground. He sat almost double—one elbow resting on his knee and his chin lying in his open hand—regaling himself with a long nine, to the no little annoyance of his neighbour.

He was a man somewhat advanced in life, with a foreign look and dress, and bore himself with that steady reserve characteristic of the Englishman.

They were soon upon the road, bnt as the Englishman stuck to his reserve, and the Yankee to his cigar, Philip gave himself up to the thoughts occasioned by the bright landscape before him ; and as it may be supposed, the first two or three miles were got over in utter silence on their part, and broken only by the occasional cracking of the driver's whip, as he urged his horses up some steep ascent, or the burst of laughter coming up from the interior of the coach, which told that the little family thrown so closely together, were making the most of their short acquaintance.

The Yankee kept on smoking his long nine, and at even intervals knocking the ashes off on the heel of his boot, until it had disappeared nearly one half of its original length ; seeming not to notice that his companions had no particular liking for its rich flavour.

About this time a turn in the road (the wind being in the right quarter) brought the full force of the cigar smoke directly across the Englishman's face. This voluminous discharge brought to bear upon the olfactory nerves of the Englishman, was more than he could withstand, and he was forced to turn away his head to keep from choking outright.

This decided indication of dislike on the part of the Englishman failed not to attract the Yankee's notice, and, taking the thing so utterly detested, and yet so much enjoyed, from his mouth, and ejecting a generous quantity of yellow saliva from ditto, over the side of the coach, he said,—

" Mebby you pertikilarly dislike smoking, mister ?"

" I am free to confess it, sir, it is very disagreeable to me, indeed."

" Ye-a-s—it is to some folks," rejoined the Yankee, and knocking the ashes from his fast disappearing long nine, he again settled down into his former position, and gave out the full compliment of smoke for the particular benefit of his unfortunate neighbours.

At this cool thrust the Englishman could ill conceal his rising temper. It was not enough that the Yankee compelled him to inhale the fumes of his villanous cigar, but he must add insult to injury ; and though one might see that he was indignant, yet he only replied,—

" You are impertinent, sir."

" That's as you may look at it, mister," said the Yankee, again removing the bone of contention from his mouth, " Du you know, Mr.—Mr.—what shall I call your name ?"

" You need not trouble yourself with it, sir."

" Oh, 'twould be no trouble, nor nothin'. But as I was saying, du you you know where I come from ?"

" From the Pigmies, for aught I care, sir."

" You never's more mistaken in your life ; but seeing we're on this pertikilar subject, I'll jest let you know I've got a sister Peggy, and a darned smart crittur she is, tu, though I say it myself. But as I was saying, more pertikilarly, Mr. ——, Mr. ——, if I might make bold of your name——"

" You can make Bold of it, if you feel so disposed, sir."

" Du tell ! I never should have thought so ! Somethin' arter the fashion of my name ; I have heard of folks being as bold as a lion. My name is Lyon, Seth Lyon. But as I was saying, Mr. Bold, I was raised up in New Hampshire, where our fathers fought and bled and died for independence and liberty, and it's a darned purty notion if one of their descendant sons can't smoke a long nine jest when he's a mind tu, and be darned to ye."

The Englishman turned away, and kept silent, thereby saying, " I shall not argue the point with you, sir ;" but whether he was convinced that the Yankee had a right to smoke in his face, does not appear.

That Seth was convinced by his own arguments was obvious, for he resumed his long nine again, and puffed away with a right good will, thereby saying " I know my rights, the rights my fathers died to establish—and I mean to maintain them."

Philip, who had witnessed the whole affair, felt half inclined to laugh, but more to be angry at Seth's determination to make himself offensive at all hazards ; and though he was in no wise implicated in the quarrel, yet as the Englishman had left the field, he would venture a word, particularly as he saw Seth was of that class who style themselves " the sovereign people," and stick pertinaciously to every prerogative that they fancy belongs to them.

" Mr. Lyon," said Erwin, in as mild a tone as he could well assume, " you have advanced sentiments here, which, if carried out in everything would have an evil influence upon society, I fear."

" I haven't advanced nothin as I knows on. I only said I had a right to smoke, and I haven't changed my mind."

Here Seth gave two or three emphatic puffs, in order to give more expression to his determination.

" No one questions your right to smoke, Mr Lyon. At the same time, we question your right to annoy others with your smoking. And this, Mr. Lyon, may apply to many other things in life. We are constituted social beings, and are daily brought into intercourse with each other. We have duties towards ourselves : we have duties to perform (as social beings) towards others. Now there are many things which we have a perfect right to do, in themselves considered, which would materially conflict with our neighbours' rights ; therefore we lose that right we otherwise have."

" I think I pertickilarly understand ye. You mean to say, I've a right to clear my mouth of this ere tobaccar spittle," (and Seth ejected the contents of his capacious mouth over the coach wheels,) " but I han't no pertickilar right to spit it into your face—hey, isn't that it ?"

" That is the way I would be understood, sir ; and though you may have a right to smoke, you have no right to strangle a man in the operation."

" Them's your pertickilar sentiments, pertickilarly expressed, eh ? well I can't zackly see why I han't a right to spit in your face, if I've a mind to ; and then you may crack me back for it, if you're a mind tu."

" For which blow you will return me another. Where will this end ?"

" That won't zackly du ; though darn me if I don't like to have everybody du as they're a mind tu. But as I ain't very opstroperlous on this occasion, there's my long nine."

With the last word, Seth hurled the cigar over the side of the coach.

" But, I say," continued Seth, looking Erwin up in the face, " you're a darned queer feller, and I should pertickilarly like to know what you are called when you're at hum ?"

Philip could hardly keep from laughing at Seth's manner of interrogating, but conquering the inclination, he replied,—

" Since I can remember, I have always been called Philip Erwin."

" And your father's name—"

" Was Philip, before me."

" I have a particular notion I knew the critter. He used to peddle tin in our parts."

" I think you have mistaken the man."

"He didn't use to sell tin-ware for old rags, and puter, and sheep skins, then? What we more partikilarly call tin pedlars."

"He had no connection with that honourable craft to my knowledge."

"Ye-a-s!—he had some sort of business, I suppose, eh? Oh, if it's anything you're ashamed on, you needn't tell me. You're going to Bosting, I calculate, On business, I s'pose?"

"Partly, sir; I shall seek to make it one of pleasure and profit."

"That's jest what I'm goin' tu du. You must know, I've got an uncle down to Bosting. He's a merchant in the hulsale and retail fish line; an all-fired big bug he is, tu. But as I was more petikilarly sayin—'

Seth was here stopped in his generous purpose of letting Erwin into a knowledge of his proposed business, by the stopping of the coach, for change of horses; but when they were upon the road again, he made a finish of it; and moreover added the history of his father, his father's father, his sister Peggy, and a score of cousins, which consumed most of the day, and the greatest share of the Englishman's small stock of patience. And when at length they arrived in the city, and Erwin was put down at the Tremont House, he bade him good-bye, hoping he might make his better acquaintance.

CHAPTER III.

THE FRIEND.

"I do not know you. Though sooth to say,
There's something in your face that reminds me,
Of things I would forget."

ON the following morning, Erwin was sitting in his room—which looked out upon Tremont-street—busy with watching the different forms and faces passing in review before him; and, guessing at the light and sad heart, by the light and shade upon the wearer's brow; at the lounger, and the man of business, and he of reckless purpose, by their different gait and bearing; when a servant entered and handed him a card.

It was a plain white card, bearing the inscription in bold letters, "John Augustus Snooksby."

"John Augustus Snooksby!" repeated Erwin, musingly. "Where have I picked that fellow up? John Augustus Snooksby! I can't recollect him! You may show the gentleman up," he said to the servant.

The servant disappeared, and soon returned, ushering in a swaggering young gentleman of twenty-five, with a small forest of black whiskers, a cap stuck aslant on his head, and a walking-stick that would have served Sampson for a battering-ram.

"Ah, my dear boy! I am delighted to see ye;" cried the man of whiskers, grasping the astonished Philip by the hand. "I saw your name on the books, and have lost not a moment in paying my respects. My dear boy, I am rejoiced at seeing you again! How are you?" and whiskers gave Erwin another most affectionate squeeze of the hand.

"Really, Mr. Snooksby—I—I am at a loss—"

"Is it possible you don't recollect me, Phil? Me your bosom friend and companion? Oh, you are quizzing me."

"By my honour, I am not."

"Don't you remember when we—pshaw! I've a great mind to be angry with you, Phil."

"If you can assist my memory—"

"D—n me, I would, if I thought you weren't joking. Don't you remember in the year 18—, when at college, of an excursion to Mount Holyoke on horseback?"

"I do. It was during the first year I was at college."

"You may remember on our return, when descending the most rugged part of the mountain, your horse stumbled and very nearly threw you over its head?"

"I kept my seat, but lost my hat down——"

"Which I recovered, and returned to you. Do you remember me now?"

"I need to apologise, sir, for not keeping in remembrance, one, to whom I acknowledge myself the debtor. But in the future, if I am permitted——"

"Oh, don't mention it, my dear fellow; the fault in part was mine. But to tell the truth, Phil, I was called home the next day, by sickness in the family, or I should have kept good the acquaintance so happily begun. *N'importe!*" he exclaimed, seating himself with all the coolness and nonchalance of a French count in his boudoir. "I think you will find me rather agreeable, of the two."

"I doubt it not, sir; and of value, too; in showing me the ways of the town. You must know, this is my first appearance."

"Command me, my dear fellow; I am completely at your disposal from this time forward. Stand on no ceremony with me, I beg. Make yourself at home. I always found it to my advantage to do so."

Snooksby leaned back in his chair and placed both his feet in the window.

"I see you have a happy faculty," said Erwin, laughing.

"Prodigious—wonderful faculty, my dear fellow. Every man is a genius;—though happily for us all, it shows itself variously. No two are noted for the same thing. Napoleon was renowned as a warrior, Francis of Valois as a libertine, Mantilini for his whiskers, Gulliver for his travels, Benjamin Franklin as a philosopher, and John Augustus Snooksby for planting himself, 'presto' like, into every parlor in Boston. So you see, Phil, you have nothing to do but to pin yourself to my sleeve, and you are the lion for the next twelve months."

"I must be dull, indeed, not to profit by the example set me. But I much mistrust my powers, sir; and why should I hope to create a sensation? There is but one sun seen; and the world has already seen——,"

This was said with the perfect seeming of an intended compliment; but there was a lurking sneer in the tone, which, if noticed at all by Snooksby, he did not see fit to acknowledge it.

"Come, come, Phil, no compliments; but let us see what we can do to pass away the morning. It now wants the half hour of twelve. Three hours and thirty minutes before dinner. Shall we take a bath? or—by Jove! Tom is out with his span of blacks!"

Snooksby threw up the window and looked out.

"A d—d splendid affair, that! perfect graces, are they not, Phil?"

Erwin looked out. A phaeton, drawn by two fine, spirited black horses, came dashing up Tremont-street, the reins in the white kid gloved hands of a young man whose dress would have entitled him to the honourable appellation of "buck of the first water."

"How are you, Tom?" shouted Snooksby from the window, as the young man reined up before the house, and was conversing with some half a dozen young bloods of the same order, who had surrounded his carriage—remarking upon the beauty of his horses, now chafing under a curbed bit. "Whither are you bound, Tom?"

"Out of town, only a short spirt;—are you engaged?"

"'Bliged to you, I am just at present. Where do you go to night; to see Julia?"

The young man coloured, and answered in the negative.

"I have no engagement for to-night."

"What do you say to the theatre?

"I will leave it to you, Snooksby," was the young man's answer, and slackening the reins over the horses' backs, they were off again, followed by the

admiring gaze of the aforesaid half-dozen young men of blood, who loudly de-
claimed against such extravagance, but were only kept from committing the like
folly themselves, by the small sum allowed them by their sires.

"He's a whole souled fellow, that Tom Freelove!" said Snooksby, turning
from the window. "You must make his acquaintance, Phil."

"So this promising youth is young Freelove, brother to the Miss Helen Freelove
that I am about to marry by my father's desire, should she consent to it," thought

Philip. "I half suspected as much. There was something in his face that seemed
familiar at first; now I see the features of the boy that was, ripened into the man
that is. He looks very much like his sister, as I remember her. Can she approve
of his life of idle extravagance? She may not. A sister can have but little
influence on a brother's actions. Yet, I marvel that a son of Colonel Freelove,
having the advantages of a virtuous sister's society, should turn out the thing I've
seen. Where does Mr. Freelove reside?" asked Erwin aloud, of Snooksby.

"In Mount Vernon-street. Do you know him, Phil?"

No. 2.

"Our fathers were neighbours, and young Freelove and myself were boys together. We were never very intimate, though; and truth to say, have not met these five years."

"And Helen?"

"I have not seen her either for the same length of time."

"You would not know her, then, my boy, she has changed wonderfully within the year."

"She is very pretty, if my memory serves me."

"Pretty says nothing for her beauty. She's a perfect Venus, Phil! Such eyes, such teeth, and such a rich neck!—enough, of themselves, to make any reasonable man go mad, not to mention her tiny hand, and prettiest ankles in the world."

"You are an adept, Mr. Snooksby, at describing beauty," said Erwin, not a little nettled at Snooksby's free use of his intended's neck and ankles.

"And when you have looked at these," continued Snooksby, "you should mark her walk the drawing-room. Such ease in her gait—such grace in every movement; equalled only by the perfect movement of Tom's black ponies. Again I say, you would not know her, Phil."

Erwin bit his lips, and felt half inclined to quarrel with Snooksby for his unheard of comparison, but, upon second thought, let it pass.

"I must accept your offer to introduce me, then. When shall it be?"

"Faith now, if it like you; our bath can await us. After that you must dine with me."

"I thank you, but——"

"Oh! it's just as well, my boy; I will dine with you, then. Allow me, I know you will."

Ringing the bell, Snooksby ordered dinner at three; and amongst numberless other things indispensable to a gentleman's table, he did not forget to mention a few bottles of favourite wine.

"We shall have the afternoon to ourselves," he said to Erwin when the servant had left the room, "and in the evening, if you feel inclined to go to the theatre, I shall have no engagement that will prevent my accompanying you."

Erwin was not a man to be imposed upon, and though he could not fail to see that Snooksby was a sort of diddler in the small way, yet he was willing to indulge him, for the sake of the amusement it afforded himself.

CHAPTER IV.

THE INTRODUCTION.

" Ye may not with a word define
The love that lightens o'er her face,
That makes her glance a glance divine,
Fresh caught from heaven, its native place—
And in her heart, as in her eye,
A spirit lovely as serene—
Makes of each charm some deity,
Well worshipp'd, though perhaps unseen."

WILL the reader follow us into one of the many splendidly furnished parlours in Mount Vernon-street? Be not over noisy, or we may disturb a young lady, who, to judge of the sullen expression of her pretty face, has had her patience tried now beyond her liking.

She was dressed for the street, and sat uneasily, tapping with her fan the blue damask cushion of the sofa. A minute after she hastened to the window and looked out.

"I wonder he comes not," she said. "He knew I expected to go out; and yet he stays away all the morning."

And then approaching one of the large mirrors that adorned the room, she scanned her face in the glass.

"I am looking frightfully to-day," she said, pettishly. "This blue does not become me. It steals the colour from my cheek, and adds a double shade under the eye. Everything plagues me this morning! My brother must go off, just as I got ready to go out, and here it is nearly one o'clock, and he's not yet returned."

At this moment the door bell rung.

"Mary, Mary, some one rings! See who it is. If it is my brother, say I have been waiting for him this hour; if any one else, I'm not at home. Do you hear? I'm not at home."

Mary went to the door, and Mr. John Augustus Snooksby crossed the threshold.

"All stuff, my dear," said Snooksby, tapping her on the mouth with his finger. "Your mistress is always at home to me and my friends. Walk up, Phil."

Snooksby began to ascend the stairs, but Erwin hesitated.

"She may not be in, as the maid says."

"No matter, I'm at home here. We'll look at the pictures in the parlour, and wait till she returns."

"What a bore that Snooksby is," said the maid, pettishly, after the style of her mistress. "I wonder Miss Helen don't cut him altogether; if she had my spirit, she would, I know."

Helen hearing footsteps on the stairs supposed it to be her brother, and was hastening to meet him, when she encountered Snooksby at the parlour-door.

"Ha! ha! ha! as I thought," roared Snooksby. "What an abominable little story-teller your Mary has got to be, Helen. I would get rid of her if I were you, if it were only to make an example of her; a warning to all future pretty ladies' maids. Do you know she insisted that you were not at home?"

"I desired her to say so, sir," said Helen, reddening, and vexed at being intruded upon by Snooksby; she was about to say something in keeping with her feelings; when, seeing Erwin, she stopped short, and coloured still deeper.

Snooksby did not notice her embarrassment.

"This is Mr. Philip Erwin," he said. "Miss Freelove, Erwin tells me you were country neighbours."

"If Miss Freelove will pardon this intrusion," said Philip, "I will promise her not to offend again. The desire to see an old playmate, has led me beyond my wonted assurance, believe me; and though I have played but a secondary part in this, I hold myself none the less censurable."

"I shall be happy to see Mr. Erwin at any hour he may favour me with a call," said Helen, frankly extending her hand to Philip, "and as for Mr. Snooksby, no one minds him. He is licensed to go where he will, like the dog I once read of, who was fed by the whole village."

"I would be angry with you, Helen, only that I know, when your tongue is most cutting, you have the most love in your heart," said Snooksby, colouring for the first time in his life.

"Just hear him! One would suppose I favour you especially, as I give you such a liberal share of tongue."

"I can prove it to you," said Snooksby, stoutly.

"Oh, I cry you mercy! I have no desire for controversy. But be seated, gentlemen; I am expecting my brother every moment. He will be glad to see you, sir," addressing herself to Erwin.

"It will give me great pleasure to renew our acquaintance. If my memory serves me, we are about the same age, twenty-two."

"My brother is but twenty, sir."

"But for the last five years, he has lived two years in one," interrupted Snooksby. "Tom is at least twenty-five."

Helen coloured at this allusion to her brother's life, which Erwin noticed, and attributed to feelings which he most desired her to have—mortification at the exposure of the idle life led by her brother, which she endured, but in no wise countenanced. Having this in his mind, he said,—

"In the country, we have but little to tempt a young man from the proscribed rules laid down and sanctioned by the old and experienced. We have our amusements, it is true; but they are, for the most part, of a character to be joined in by the young and the old. Hence it is that one seldom lives faster than another. We have no great dinners to glut a pampered appetite, and thereby injure health; consequently we grow not older than one year succeeds another; nor live two years in one, as Mr. Snooksby would have it. But still, Miss Freelove, we of the country—one that likes to dwell there from choice; a thinking man—one that loves to stray over cultivated fields, and witness God in every unfolding blade and flower—will grow sage in feelings, if not in looks."

"Bravo, Phil! a most excellent discourse, and well pointed, withal. It will give me great pleasure to listen to another of the same sort and tenour; but not now, my boy—in the afternoon, when I have drunk your excellent wine, and got ready for a doze."

Erwin took no notice of Snooksby's words, and Helen said,—

"I cannot say I love the country. 'Tis well enough for men, for they have a hundred out of door amusements, which we poor souls have not. How could a young lady amuse herself in the country; by firing stones at birds?"

"If she like it, she may; so she does not harm them. But I am of the opinion, that an afternoon's sail on some one of our little lakes would be quite as agreeable to her."

"That would do for to-day; what for to-morrow?"

"A ride on horseback."

"And the next day?"

"If nothing better offers, she may fill her basket, and visit her poor neighbours. We have enough of them, indeed; and believe me, their grateful looks will be an abundant reward for the little it may cost her; and such thanks will warm and gladden her heart more than all the gay scenes man has invented."

Their discourse was here broken off by the entrance of young Freelove.

"Tom," cried Snooksby, "you are just in the nick of time, unless you wish to lose your sister. My friend Erwin, here, is trying to inflame Helen with a proper love for the country, as he styles it. Be sure he has some design in it all."

"Brother, this is Mr. Erwin, of S——ville; you ought to remember him."

"Perfectly, and most heartily do I welcome him under my roof."

The two young men shook each other heartily by the hand.

A half hour passed in general conversation, touching the amusements of the day, &c., &c., and Erwin and Snooksby took their leave; Snooksby having previously arranged, however, to have Erwin invite them all to the theatre in the evening.

"Now what do you think of her?" asked Snooksby, as soon as they were in the street.

"I see nothing of my country neighbour in the city belle."

"Well, what do you think of the city belle?"

"That she is most fair."

"You are devilish cool about it, Phil. Is, 'she is most fair,' all you have to say in her praise?"

"Really Mr. Snooksby ——"

"Oh, don't distress yourself, my boy; if her beauty has power to elicit to stronger expressions, she is not for my market. But really, Phil, had she been to you what she is to me ——"

" Am I to—to understand that—that——"

" Why, it was not exactly settled," said Snooksby, carelessly. " In fact I never offered myself; why should I? What the deuce could I do with a wife? Nevertheless, it was well understood by both of us."

Philip Erwin was more thoughtful after this conversation with Snooksby.

" Helen," said Freelove, when Erwin and Snooksby had left the house, " how would you like your old playmate for a husband?"

" Vastly!—but I had liked it much better if you had come home in season to have gone out with me."

" But seriously ,sis."

" Seriously then, I do not like him."

" The reason, pray?"

" The reason?—reasons, rather!"

" Well——?"

" In the first place, then, he wears no moustache, which in a gentleman is unpardonable, being like a cat without ears. Lacking that necessary appendage, he is less than a man; and being less than a man, he is no man for me."

" Give him three months with the aid of a little macassar, and he will show you as brilliant a moustache as ever laid siege to a woman's heart."

" Then he prides himself upon his superior literary acquirements; and before he is with you a five minutes' time, will give you an ' inkling,' to say the least, of his remarkable powers of mind; which, if rendered into pure English, would say, ' few men are my equal.' When I give up my liberty, it shall be to a man, and nothing more."

" You little minx! if you have done with your finding fault, we will have a little matter of fact discourse. I have to tell you that of all that immense fortune left us by our father, there is not enough to keep my horses in provender for six months."

"I have heard it for the twentieth time, brother."

"I can scarcely realise it; only five short years," said Freelove, gloomily. " Five years ago, I believed our wealth inexhaustible; to-day I have been asked for money I borrowed of a friend, and had not a dollar to pay it with."

" Will not old Ned supply you?"

" Yes, as long as I can give him two dollars in collateral, for every dollar that he loans me. D——n him! he's got everything now."

" I think he would let me have the money."

" Why should he let you have the money, Helen?" asked Freelove, sharply.

Helen coloured, and replied, " I only guessed he might be persuaded to let me have some."

" Persuasion would as soon split a rock! And then, that fellow, Ryeface, is making a touse about the paltry sum of two hundred dollars, which I owe him for the keeping of my horses; and then there's Tightlace ——"

" Why not dispose of your horses, brother?"

" Will you give up your waiting maid?"

" That is a very different thing."

" Oh, very, then there's your shawl that cost five hundred dollars, and a set of jewels, seven hundred more, ordered last week. But as you say ' that is a very different thing,' don't ask me to give up my horses, Helen. If we commence, we might as well give up everything—our houses and servants."

Helen turned pale.

" What can we do, brother?"

" You must save us, Helen!"

" How is it to be done?"

" Marry Erwin."

" Brother!"

" I repeat, marry Erwin,"

" Are you mad?"

" You may have him if you will."

" You talk strangely, brother.'

" I talk the sober truth.   You have but to use a little art, and he is yours. He is taken with you already."

" How foolishly you talk, brother."

Helen feigned to be offended at her brother's words, but in truth her vanity had whispered as much before.

" Use your best endeavours and I promise you success," said Freelove, decidedly.

" I cannot love him, brother."

" Throw love into the fire!   You have no aversion to five thousand a year, for pin money, I imagine."

" Then he will prove such a tyrant, and will not let me stir from home, except I ——"

" But without him you will have no home at all.   I tell you, Helen, Erwin's princely fortune alone, will enable us to maintain our present position.   Without him I must give up my dinners and supper parties and horse-races, and above all, my beautiful blacks.   You will have to give up this house, with all its servants, your shawl and jewels, your ——"

" Say no more, brother, were he physic, I would swallow him down to save our reputation."

Freelove now felt easier than he had for months.   He had witnessed the dwindling away of that immense fortune left him by his father, with feelings amounting to despair; yet he could see no way by which he could curtail his expenses, and thereby save himself from utter ruin.   Economy was a word he knew not of, and he kept on his prodigality until beggary stared him full in the face.

Still he drove on his blacks, and to all appearances, was the same rich "Tom Freelove," happy and courted by society, up to the day he was introduced to the reader.

On this day he had received a letter from his confidential attorney in the country, with intelligence that purposed to put him on his legs again. This piece of intelligence, said attorney gleaned from James, the old servant of the late Philip Erwin; viz , that on his dying bed, the old gentleman had made his son promise to wed the daughter of his old friend, Helen Freelove, should it prove agreeable to the wishes of the lady.

CHAPTER V.

THE PLAY.

Polonius.	My lord, I have news to tell you.
Hamlet.	My lord, I have news to tell you. When Roscius was an actor in Rome,—
Polonius.	The actors are come hither my lord.
Hamlet.	Buz, buz!
Polonius.	Upon my honour,—
Hamlet.	Then came each actor on his ass,—

FEW men can look upon a beautiful woman without emotion.   There is something of witchery attending her, even in her most wayward mood; but when beauty has the attributes of virtue. modesty and gentleness, like a halo lighting up her divine features, she throws around her a spell that binds all within her influence with chains stronger than iron.   Proud lords! ye are an easy prey! and oftentimes a willing one.

Philip was not in love with Helen Freelove, for with him love must be the work of time; but he was enchanted with her grace; captivated by her beauty.   He was pleased with the idea of possessing a woman of such rare beauty, but still this would pass for nothing—the rich casket would possess but few attractions, wanting its richest jewel, a good heart. That she should be a little giddy and wild, he thought natural enough, being the effect of education and association ; but beneath this, he hope to find a true woman's heart.

Snooksby's assertion of their attachment staggered him not a little. Was she partial to Snooksby? Nothing more likely. Snooksby was a bold reckless fellow ; and these qualifications might be the desired ones, and the surest guarantee to a fashionable lady's heart. Well, if she prefers him, let her go, he thought. I do not love her ; and with all my trying, I am not sure that I could. But I will keep the promise I made my father, and leave the rest to her.

When Erwin and his party arrived at the theatre, they found it crammed to overflowing. The theatre-going people were enjoying a season of rare dramatic feasting, by the nightly performance of the two Boston favourites, Tree and Forrest.

On this night was to be represented Bulwer's "Lady of Lyons ; or Love and Pride." Miss Tree was to appear as Pauline, and Mr. Forrest as Claude, supported by a powerful company.

It wanted some minutes to the rising of the curtain when our party arrived ; which time was pretty generally seized upon by all present, to see how his or her neighbour was dressed.

Here, was pointed out a young miss, just from a boarding-school ; who, as the phrase goes, " had just come out," accompanied by her mother and father. There, a buxom widow, who has but now put off her weeds of a year's endurance, surrounded by a score of bachelors ; she the sun—the centre of the system ; they the planets moving in their respective orbits, according as she favours them, taking their l ght and motion from her, the lovely centre.

On the extreme right, erect, standing with his back against the boox-door, in view of the whole assemblage, was a man deliberately surveying the audience through an opera-glass, end feasting his eyes upon the choice bits of beauty coming in the range of his vision. A hundred other glasses were in active operation, though less prominently located :—

"All a quizzing; quiz, quiz, quizzing."

And those that were not so fortunate as to possess an opera-glass, neither a quiz zing glass, quizzed with those instruments of a more ancient invention, which they all fortunately brought with them.

Snooksby, who was known to every ninety-nine out of the hundred, was engaged in conversation with two ladies in the next box. One was an elderly lady who once had laid claim to considerable beauty ; and now her intelligent features were marked with a mild and benevolent expression that would have rendered her face an object of interest, were it not that at her side sat one of the loveliest of earth's lovely daughters.

She seemed to be the star of the evening ; and glasses from all parts of the house were directed at the box in which she sat, as if by universal consent. She seemed not to notice it, however, but kept up a spirited and easy conversation with Snooksby.

One of the most attentive observers of that box was a man about fifty years of age, whom Erwin at once recognised as the Englishman, his fellow-traveller on the day he reached the city. He was the same, yet not the same. His cold exterior —the manifest indifference he exhibited towards everything had given place to excitement, equalled only by his former coldness ; and his pale face, almost ghastly in its expression, and his inquiring eyes, rendered him an object of much remark.

Helen meanwhile was all mirth and gaity, and continued to hold possession of Erwin's ear, and kept up a sprightly conversation, assisted by Freelove.

The curtain went up.

The first act is over ; and the audience, who throughout had maintained a perfect lence, spell-bound by the acting of the two master spirits of the play, were again t at liberty. Erwin looked for the Englishman, but he was no where to be en.

"How do you like the heroine?" asked Helen of Erwin.

"With your leave, I will defer giving my opinion until the play is over. We hould not be over hasty in forming an opinion. No character is understood in an our. I have read of those who were eminently disagreeable, proving in the end a arden of rich fruit and flowers. Of others, again, who were the most agreeable— s fair as fancy could dream of, seemingly as pure as the otol flower ; but who, like he otol, at heart conceal a poisonous serpent. This Pauline at first appears faulty, ut she may display feelings hereafter, that shall wholly redeem her character."

Helen did not venture a reply, for she would have differed with Erwin, and called aults, her greatest virtue, namely, pride, love of display, and a desire to bring ll to her feet.

Freelove and Snooksby had left the box at the falling of the curtain, to take "wherewith to brace the outward man." They would have invited Erwin, only hat they knew that he would refuse them. They now returned, having in their company a young man the perfect embodiment of a furnishing-shop, perfumed to his finger's ends.

"How , do, Miss Freelove?" he drawled out in a tone that would have done Mantilini credit, leaning forward in the box to the annoyance of several worthy people. "I kiss your fair hand, I do, by my faith."

"What brings you here to-night, Mr. Slickham?" asked Helen, "I thought you would be at the H—'s."

"Do you ask, when their party lacked its only attraction? For no other cause came I away ; true—by my faith, How shall I account for Miss Freelove's not bein g there?"

"Also for the want of attraction," said Helen laughing. "Let me present to you Mr. Erwin—Mr. Slickham."

Slickham extended to Erwin the two forefingers of his right hand, and with his left hand brought a quizzing-glass to his eye, and looked Philip over from head to foot.

"Extremely happy to make your acquaintance, Mr. Erwin, I am, by my faith. Just from the country, I suppose?"

"A natural supposition, Mr. Slickham ; and keeping up the supposition, I suppose you are from some country beyond seas?" said Philip, coolly surveying Slickham in turn.

"Mistake—quite a mistake, Mr. Erwin. A palpable mistake, by my faith. I am a Bostonian."

"You astonish me beyond measure!"

"A fact, by my faith! as any of my friends will testify."

"I will believe any impossibility after this! I learned, it is true, by a Boston paper that reached us a few years since, that a Captain —— had imported several rare specimens of the Ourang-outang, but I had not the faintest idea that they could be grown in this country."

Slickham, who was still regarding Erwin through his glass, now dropped his under jaw, and opened his eyes to their utmost width in speechless astonishment. A laugh from Snooksby brought him to himself, and turning round, he coolly remarked,—

"Past my comprehension, by my faith!" and then making his bow to Helen, joined Snooksby at the box-door. For the first time his eyes fell on the fair stranger in the next box.

"A Hebe, a very Hebe! by my faith," he exclaimed. "Do you mark, Snooksby? Is she not divine?"

"Your highest praise would beggar her rich beauty, my boy! Did you never see her before?"

"Never, by my faith! Who is she?"

"Annie, one of the orphans of St. Mary; the protege of Madame Jerome, its founder, that respectable old lady sitting by her side."

"You tell me wonders! It is deuced strange I never have seen her before. It is, by my faith."

"Not in the least; this is the first evening the old lady has taken her out."

"You are acquainted with her, then!"

"Intimately."

"By my faith, you shall introduce me, Snooksby."

ERWIN AND HIS PARTY AT THE THEATRE.

"And for what purpose? If you think to make a conquest there, you are too late. She has already disposed of her heart."

"You astonish me; you do by my faith."

Slickham again brought the glass to his eye, and drank draughts of beauty from her sweet face.

"Aurora broke not upon the world, the first morn of creation, with half the raedience she appears in to-night! A perfect Venus, by my faith! And you tell m—she is engaged!"

No. 3.

"Why, we are not exactly engaged; although, as I said before, I have her heart. But then she is so young; and Madame Jerome, too; though she is set upon the marriage, I do believe she would break her heart at losing her. And so——"

"Are you—Snooksby!—you the happy—you astonish me, you do, by my faith!"

"If you love me, Slickham, don't let it go any further. We keep it as close as possible. But as you were inclined to make advances—you understand, in consideration of our friendship, I thought I would spare you the mortification of a refusal. That was all."

"You are very kind; you are, by my faith."

Snooksby entered the box, and seated himself where he could hold the fair Annie in conversation, and Slickham, heaving a sigh that threatened to disturb the smooth folds of his shirt bosom, hastened to another part of the house, to get a better view of Annie.

The play was one which presented some of the strongest points of excellence and nobleness in the human character—drawing the hero and heroine into a vortex that threatened to shipwreck their only chance of happiness, which was forced upon the imagination by the incomparable genius of a Tree and Forrest, calculated to awaken a feeling of deep interest on the part of the audience.

Erwin in some of the most touching scenes, glanced at his fair neighbour in the next box. Her eyes were moist with tears, her bosom heaved with the intensity of her feelings, and the whole expression of her face was one of heartfelt sympathy. He could but compare her expressive countenance with the beautiful but cold face of Helen Freelove. Her eyes were directed to the stage; she was silent and attentive, but there was wanting that fine expression that tells of a feeling heart. Man loves sympathy in a woman.

It was in that part of the play in which Pauline discovers she has been duped; and Claude describes the wild love that urged him to commit the wrong his better feelings cried out against, in the following beautiful and touching language:—

"Pauline, by pride angels have fallen ere thy time; by pride—
That sole alloy of thy most lovely mould—
The evil spirit of a bitter love,
And a revengeful heart had power upon thee.
From my first years, my soul was filled with thee;
I saw thee midst the flow'rs the lowly boy
Tended, unmark'd by thee—a spirit of bloom,
And joy, and freshness; as if spring itself
Were made a living thing, and wore thy shape!
I saw thee, and the passionate heart of a man
Entered the breast of the wild dreaming boy;
And from that hour I grew—what to the last
I shall be—thine adorer! Well, this love,
Vain, frantic, guilty, if thou wilt, became
A fountain of ambition and bright hope.
I thought of tales that by the winter hearth
Old gossips tell—how maidens sprung from kings,
Have stoop'd from their high sphere; how love, like death,
Levels all rank, and lays the shepherd's crook
Beside the sceptre. Thus I made my home
In the soft palace of a fairy future!
My father died; and I, the peasant-born,
Was my own lord. Then did I seek to rise
Out of the prison of my mean estate;
And, with such jewels as the exploring mind
Brings from the caves of knowledge, buy my ransom
From those twin gaolers of the daring heart—
Low birth and iron fortune. Thy bright image,
Glass'd in my soul, took all the hues of glory,
And lured me on to those inspiring toils

By which man masters man. For thee I grew
A midnight student o'er the dreams of sages!
For thee I sought to borrow from each grace,
And every muse, such attributes as lend
Ideal charms to love. I thought of thee,
And passion taught me poesy—of thee
And on the painter's canvass grew the life
Of beauty ! Art became the shadow
Of the dear starlight of thy haunting eyes !
Men called me vain—some mad ;—I heeded not,
But stilled toiled on—hoped on—for it was sweet
If not to win, to feel more worthy thee !"

During this recital, into which the artist threw his whole soul, the audience were hushed into stillness almost startling. Just then, when Pauline, equally carried away by his eloquent appeal—like as no eyes were looking on, puts the question to her innermost being,—

'Has he a magic to exorcise hate ?'

a scream broke on the ear, like an electric shock, startling every one in the full audience from their seats. Erwin saw that the elderly lady, in the company of the lovely stranger that had occupied no small share of his thoughts, notwithstanding the exciting character of the play, had fainted.

In the general confusion, nothing was being done for her recovery. Instantly perceiving it, Erwin, followed by Snooksby, sprang over the slight partition that divided the boxes, and bore her to the open air, In a few moments, from the coolness of the night air, she opened her eyes, and springing to her feet, caught her young companion—who was leaning over her, rubbing her hands, and by every means in her power, trying to bring her back to consciousness—and folding her in her arms, looked wildly about her, as if to shield her from some impending danger.

"What do you fear, dear mother ?" asked the girl, trying to release herself from the firm grasp of the terrified woman, " no one will harm us."

" Did you not see him ?" she asked wildly.

" Who, mother ? There is no one here but Mr. Snooksby, and—and——"

" There are none but friends, here," said Erwin, soothingly. " You have nothing to fear."

" No one here—friends—I thank you, gentlemen," she said, still very much excited, and then, seeing several men on the side walk, at no great distance from them, she hurried Annie towards the carriage. " Where is Sambo ? We will go home, Annie."

" Here I is, missa ; I'se on hand like the reggelar Day and Martin. Yah, yah !"

Erwin and Snooksby assisted the ladies into their carriage ; and as it drove off, they caught the speaking eyes of Annie, thanking them for their offices.

As Erwin turned to enter the theatre, he saw a man entering a carriage. It drove off. Erwin got but a glimpse of his pale face in the dim light of the lamp, but he thought (he was not sure) it was the Englishman.

Order had been restored, and the play was going forward, when Erwin and Snooksby took their seats in the box ; and all present had apparently forgotten the little incident that had for a moment interrupted their amusement. But Erwin could not dismiss it from his thoughts. The alarm of the lady, her strange actions and wild expressions in connection with the pale and agitated Englishman ; and above all, the sweet, expressive face of the young girl, made impressions not easily forgotten. And when the play was over, and he had retired to his chamber, her dark, tearful eyes followed him in mournful silence ; and falling asleep, he dreamed he was thrown upon some desolate rocks, where the sea broke in fearful surges, and the wind sported in wild revelry. All was dark, turbulent, and wild beneath ; above was the clear sky, studded with numberless stars, and as he gazed upward into the spangled vault, each shining world became so many loving eyes, that smiled confidently in love.

CHAPTER VI.

ST. MARY.

"It is a story's picture; we must group
So that the eye may see what the quick mind
Has chronicled before.   The painter's art
Is twin unto a poet's—both were born,
That truth might have a tone of melody,
And fancy shape her motion into grace."

ON one of the principal roads, five miles distant from the city, stands St. Mary. You approach it from the highway, by a broad gravelled walk, almost shut out from the sun by rows of lofty trees.   The asylum stood on high ground, which sloped off at an easy grade for some rods, till it met a wood of various trees surrounding the house, among which Evelyn might have delighted to roam, but in truth they were so thickly woven, that the sun seldom, if ever, penetrated to the paths beneath.

Most of those paths were narrow, only of sufficient width for two to walk abreast.   There were others wider indeed, and gravelled; and at intervals rude seats were placed, where the curious visitor might rest himself, or where the contemplative man could pause and reflect upon the past, or speculate upon the future; or where, which was most generally the case, indeed, the young orphans of St. Mary could dress their dolls, protected from the burning sun by the thick canopy of green leaves above.

In front of the asylum, as we have said, stretches a lawn several rods in extent; in the rear, a garden, tastefully laid out, where the young girl could cull a rose or jessamine for her hair, or the maiden gather a bouquet to adorn her room.

The asylum was a plain brick edifice, of considerable extent, built solely for the purpose which it answered, viz., an asylum for the orphans whom God has mysteriously, though we trust, in love, deprived of that earthly support, its natural protection—a retreat for the innocent victim of unlawful love, who is ushered into this world a stranger child, without a name; left to the cold charities of an uncharitable world, which not unfrequently points to the little outcast, as if it was guilty of its own existence.   It was built to shelter the unfortunate, and not to tickle the eye with Egyptian, Grecian, Gothic or modern Pantamorphican architectural beauty.   It was built for usefulness, and not for show.

It was a square built edifice, and to give light and air to the greatest number of sleeping rooms, the middle of the building was left a hollow square, in the centre of which played a fountain; and near at hand were erected baths, for the accommo dation of all.   Nothing was wanting, throughout the establishment, to further the comfort and happiness of those for whom it was designed.

Shut out from the world, the little orphans lived, scarcely dreaming that there was aught of this earth save their little garden, sloping lawn, and many pathed wood beyond.   From the top of the asylum, indeed, they had a view beyond the wood.

The city was seen in the distance, with its glittering spires and domes.   Charles River, a speck on the landscape, lay like a thread of silver, reflecting the clouds, as they chased each other along; splendid villas and comfortable farm houses were thickly scattered at every point, and orchards and richly cultivated fields, changing in prospect with morning and mid-day, sunset and moonlight—was a scene their little hearts joyed to look upon; and with contented hearts they looked forward to the day when they should be of sufficient age to accompany their kind potroness beyond the walls of their safe retreat.

The sun had descended about two hours from the meridian, but the day was still warm and bright. There had been a shower in the morning, but it cleared off before noon, and left nature but the fresher, and the wood more green, and the flowers in the garden more bright and full of perfume. Groups of little girls were scattered over the lawn, making the wood echo with their joyous laughter, and maidens seated under the shade of the wood, intent upon their afternoon lessons. All was sunshine and flowers, and was as smiling as the spring time of youth.

At this hour a young maiden might have been seen leaving the asylum with a book in her hand, and entering the wood. She passed down a gravelled walk till she came to a small chapel, joined to a patch of ground scooped out of the thick wood, where the sun looked smilingly upon five small mounds, which told that the like number of little orphans, that had been welcomed to St. Mary, had been called home, and their dust rested in this peaceful spot, with the song of birds in the green boughs above. Near to this was a small pond of water, of muddy bottom and shallow depth.

Seating herself on a rude bench near the chapel, she removed a cape bonnet from her head, revealing a face as fair and bright as a poet's dream. We say she was fair; nay, she was beautiful! and there we stop. To speak of the soft velvet of her cheeks, her ruby lips, like twin rosebuds laid together—aquiline nose—eyes dark blue—in smiles or tears equally beautiful! arching brows, slightly pencilled on a forehead white and smooth as mother-of-pearl, adorned with flowing hair, dark as night—would be to echo what has been said of a hundred quite as fair as she; yet she was most beautiful!

Laying the bonnet on the bench beside her, she opened the book in her hand, and as she perused its pages, the expression of her face, which was but the mirror of her soul, bore witness that the work was of thrilling interest.

She had been occupied thus but a few minutes when footsteps near caused her to start. Her face became instantly flushed, and starting from the seat, she was leaving the spot, but almost instantly she turned back again, and gave her hand to the object of her dread.

It was a young man, weak and diminutive in body, with a pale girlish face; an eye full and soft, denoting a mild, even temper; broad, intelligent forehead; showing that while the mind lived and flourished with powerful strength, it fed upon the body, which sickened in proportion as the mind developed.

"I will not detain you, Annie," he said, in a low, musical voice, "I see you would avoid me."

"Charles—I——"

"Nay, 'tis past, and I will forgive it. It is no marvel that you do not love me, Annie; for I have not the form or stature of a man. I have the feelings of a man, Annie; can eat, can act, can think, and love as a man; but what signify these, wanting the essential man? I may not hope for thy love, but I did hope you felt for me the love of a sister—that my presence was not altogether hateful to you."

"I do love and respect you as a brother, Charles, but you have of late——"

"I have, indeed, been bold and presumptuous. I have troubled you too often with my unwelcome love. I have forced you to listen when I should have known it was tiresome to thee. Truly love is blind and foolish, and selfish withal. I will have done with this, Annie; I will be silent as you could wish; I will school my eyes to express less of admiration in thy sight; will teach my heart to lie still at thy approach; will do anything—so I lose not thy friendship; am denied not thy presence."

Annie's eyes filled with tears.

"Forgive me, Charles," she said, "forgive me, that I cannot love you. The time may come when I shall feel differently; now I love no one but—but——"

She hesitated.

"You do love, then? Pray God you may not love hopelessly, Annie."

"Yes, I love Madame Jerome more than any other earthly being," she saip regaining her self-possession. "Without being my mother, she has been a dear mother, instructress, and a true friend. She took me in a little outcast, clothed, educated, and gave me a happy home, and all done so cheerfully, that I almost ceased to remember I was a dependent upon her bounty. For all this she asks no return ; and, to say the truth, I have nothing to give, save the love you would rob her of," she said, with a smile.

"Nay, not so, Annie. The love I seek would nothing take from a mother's love. It is of a kind——"

"No more of this, Charles, I beg. It is an unhappy theme, and for the sake of us both should be forgotten."

"Forgetfulness comes not here, Annie, but I will seem to forget; and for the future you shall have no cause to complain of me. I see your man coming this way, and I will leave you. But, Annie, for the future do not seek to shun me. Give me some small portion of your leisure moments ; it will cost you nothing, and to me such occasional draughts will prove the antidote of life."

Charles moved away, while Annie, taking one of the by-paths which we mentioned in the first of this chapter, sought the asylum.

"Good, kind, noble, generous heart," she said, when stopping in the garden to pick a rose. "Why is it I do not love him ? He possesses every quality that should entitle him to be loved ; and yet my foolish heart refuses to love him. I love him as a brother," she continued, after a moments silence, in which pity held the largest share of her thoughts. "How I loved to listen to the low melody of his voice, when seated upon the lawn, when the stars were out, and he discoursed of them so eloquently. We were happy, then," she continued, her eyes filling with tears. "But he must talk of love and spoil it all. I told him I could love him only as a sister ; and I know not how it is, since that night I went to the theatre, my feelings have strangely changed towards him. I no longer have a relish for his society. I fear I am very foolish ; I wish it were otherwise."

Thus freeing her mind in part, of its heavy load, she entered the Asylum.

Of Charles McIver, the unhappy young man whom we have but now introduced to the reader, we shall say a few words and then close the chapter. He was the son of Luther McIver, Professor of Languages at Harvard College. From a child he was weak and suffering in body, but gave tokens of a strong, healthy and vigorous mInd.

He was not like other boys, fond of amusements common to the age ; but preferred rather to be alone by himself, poring over his books, under some tree in the college grounds. When older he cared less for books, and clung more to his own thoughts. For whole days he would be absent from his home, treading the silent aisles of Mount Auburn, and there with the dead around, perchance viewless spirits,

> "Astray from their forgotten habitude of clay."

with their low spirit sounds whispering in his ears ; revolving some favourite scheme for man's advancement and happiness. He wished to be alone, but that was no mark of selfishness, for,——

> "He that dwelleth mainly by himself, heedeth most of others,
> But they that live in crowds think chiefly of themselves ;
> There is indeed a selfish seeming, where the anchorite liveth alone,
> But probe his thoughts—they travel far, dreaming for ever of the world.
> And there is an apparent generosity when a man mixeth freely with his fellows,
> But prove his mind, by day and night, his thoughts are all of self.

One day when he was scarce twelve years old, Charles in some of his walks chanced to enter the grounds of St. Mary. Its quiet wood and gravelled aisles just suited his lonely feelings. Leaving the main walk that would have led him to the asylum, he took a narrow path on the left, which he followed admiringly for some distance, when a vision broke upon him that riveted him to the spot.

Upon a rude bench just before him was a young girl. Her back was towards him, but she occasionally turned her head, so he got a profile view of her face; and boy as he was, he had dreamed of a Hippodame, Camilla, and Atalanta—had an ideal little short of perfection; and in the bright being before him he saw it realised. Something engaged her attention—her little hands were employed with some work to him unknown. The desire to know what could interest so fair a being in such a place, caused him to take a step forward for a nearer view, when stepping thoughtlessly on some dry brushwood, the noise startled the wood-nymph to her feet.

Charles saw he was discovered, and beating a retreat, hid himself behind a tree; but to no purpose. The little girl, putting down the doll she was dressing, and which so much puzzled the youthful philosopher, clapped her tiny hands and hastened after him.

"Come forth, Sir Curiosity," she said pertly. "Come forth, I say! It would be a pity that so much pains should go unrewarded."

Charles suffered himself to be led forward by the fair girl, his eyes all the while doing the grace his tongue refused to utter.

"So you took all this trouble to see me dress my doll, did you?" she said, blushing under his steady gaze. "One would think you never saw a doll. No matter—you can be of service to me; so I will not scold you. I was just wishing I had some one to hold the doll for me, while I put her hair on."

"Thy wishes must ever, like a holy prayer, command the special favour of Providence. He hath sent me at thy wish."

"Be careful, Mr. Curiosity; you are too rough! If you lay hold of her in that way you will tumble her dress. Gentlemen should not treat ladies in that manner. Smooth down her frock. That will do better."

Charles could not suppress a smile at her artless manner, and said,—

"I have been little used to the society of ladies, which must plead my excuse for so much rudeness. Do you come here every day to dress your doll?"

"Yes; except when Madame Jerome desires me not to. Do you come here every day, too?"

"I knew not there was such a place till within the hour. Shall I come every day?"

"You did not ask leave to come now," she said, archly, "and you can do as you like about coming again."

The reader need not be told where Charles passed the most of the leisure or how in time he learned to love, nay, idolise, the little Annie.

CHAPTER VII.

THE LETTER.

"The world's all title-page, there's no contents;
 The world's all face; the man who shows his heart
 Is hooted for his nudities and scorned."

WHEN Charles McIver left Annie, he hastened down the walk, and was passing the individual who had interrupted their unhappy discourse, but was detained by him.

"Hou'd du, Mr. ——, let me see, your name's Charles?"

"It is."

"I thought so; but it isn't to be expected I can pertikilarly remember all the names here-a-bouts in only three days, which I have been in this 'ere place. I have got a letter here for Miss Annie. I seed she was with you a minute ago, but clipped it when she seed me coming. Her steps is as uncertain as a red squirrel's. Mebby you can tell me where she's stirred her traps?"

"She has returned to the asylum, as I think."

"You think so? Ye-a-s—but I say, Mr. Charles, you look rather streaked."

"How do you mean?"

"How? Why—you look pertikilarly kind of peak-ed pindlin' like—I guess you aint well."

"I never enjoy very good health."

"Du tell us! But I guess I can't stop a talkin' long. Good-bye, I guess I shall get a little acquainted with ye a bit."

Thus saying, Seth hastened to deliver his letter. He met Annie in the hall, having just left Madame Jerome, who had not quitted her room since the evening of her visit to the theatre, from indisposition occasioned by the fright then received, and the cause of which she refused to explain to any one.

Annie manifested much surprise on receiving the note. It was written on very fine English paper, gilt-edged; and addressed to the "Beautiful Annie of St. Mary."

"It smells allfired strong of musk," said Seth, making up a wry face.

Annie opened the note, and as she hastily run over its contents, her face expressed still greater surprise, not unmingled with anger. As the reception this note met with had some influence upon the actions of a certain individual hereafter to be disclosed, we will give it to the reader. The style of the hand was remarkably neat, and read thus :—

"MOST ADORABLE OF YOUR SEX,—Since the evening when first my admiring eyes fell on thy matchless beauty; my heart has been full of nought but thee. Since I heard the sweet tone of thy melodious voice, all other voices (before passing sweet) fall on my ear harsh and discordantly. Since I saw the perfect symmetry of thy fairy-like hand, all other hands have no charms for me; not the least, by my faith.

"I pass through the crowded halls, where beauty holds her court; smiling eyes flash up to mine invitingly; but in all, I see not the witchery of thy melting orbs —nor the winning grace, nor the peerless form of my beautiful Annie; all true, by my faith.

"I say my Annie—for I have made up my mind to marry you; I have, by my faith. What does it signify that I am at the head of the elite of our city—that I have gold to buy every pleasure man could sigh for—and you but a poor orphan girl? History gives us repeated instances in which great men have stooped for love. With their example before me, then, I make you a free tender of my hand, as you have my heart; I do, by my faith. Let us, dear Annie, make each other blest by a mutual interchange of vows; and for that purpose, meet me this evening at nine o'clock, in the broad avenue leading from the road; and then we will further consult our future happiness.

"Till then, believe me truly,
"Your ever-faithful friend and admirer,
"TIGHTLACE SLICKHAM."

"Was there ever anything half so foolish and insulting as this letter?" she exclaimed, when she had read it through, almost ready to weep with vexation.

"I can tell better when I've hearn it," said Seth in reply. "It was a darned fired slick feller what brought it anyhow. He was pertikilarly anxious tu have me say tu you, that he was waitin' for the answer."

"Does he expect an answer to this insulting epistle?"

"Tu be sure he does, and the critter's waitin' down by the bars now for it. If you han't no pertikilar desire to write, let me read it, and I'll give him a glister."

"Such arrogance deserves but one answer," she said, handing the note to Seth, after sealing it.   "You may give that to the man in waiting."

"Why, this is the letter he brought."

"'Tis all the answer it requires, good Seth.   Do as I desire you."

"This affair is pertikilarly curious," muttered Seth, leaving the room.

Annie hastened to her chamber, threw herself into a chair, and burst into tears.

"It must be he," she thought.   "It can be no one else.   I saw his eyes fixed

upon me several times in the course of the evening, but they were respectful.   He looked not that vain, foolish thing this note bespeaks him.   'Meet me this evening to consult our future happiness.'   So ran the letter.   I have no patience!   To think he should have such a low opinion of me. Meet him!   To presume so much. because, forsooth! he came to mother's assistance, and helped us to our carriage. He would not have dared to write, if I had not been an orphan, which he so basely alludes to in his letter," and her tears started afresh.

No. 4.

no better.   His letter throughout shows but a shallow mind ; and he is more deserving of pity than contempt.   Oh, what a mistake was there !   To form a being so perfect in all that meets the eye, and for the mind give but a counterfeit.   I will not think any more of him.   If he had but Charles's noble mind !   Dear Charles, I never had one insulting word or look from you.   Oh, would I could feel the same for you I have felt for this man.   I did right to send him back his letter —I will not see him, never, never !"

But we must leave Annie to her bitter insulted feelings, and follow Seth Lyon to deliver the returned note.   He found the man at the gate or bars, as he styled it, waiting for an answer.   Hastening up to him, he said,—

"Do you see this piece of paper ?"

"Is it the note I gave you to give to the person to whom it is addressed ?"

"Ye-a-s ; and that 'ere person addressed considers herself purty considerably insulted."

"Insulted ?"

"Ye-a-s ; insulted !   I only wish I know'd what's inside, that's all !   And though its pertikilarly gin the nateral laws of God and man, I'd make daylight shine through your musk-rat.   Whew ! just smell of that."

And Seth handed the note, which gave such evidence of Mr. Slickham's taste in perfumery, but which, nevertheless, shocked Seth's olfactory nerves beyond endurance, to the man.

"Sir ! this language——"

"Oh, don't you go for to be obstroperlous ; or I'll give you a small taste of what I've got laid up for Mr. Muskrat."

And Seth doubled up his huge fist, like unto a sledge-hammer, and advanced on the man, who made off, muttering something not very Christian-like, and which, luckily for him, did not reach Seth's ears.

"There goes an allfired coward !   he, he !   he thought I'se going to strike him.   I'd a great mind tu du it, that's sartain ; if it's only tu give him a taste of the true New Hampshire flesh and grit.   It would be a hard bit for him to swaller, I'm thinkin'.   He !   he !   he !"   and Seth held up his delicate hand, and regarded it with evident delight.

"Now I bet a pound of maple sugar jest out of the kittle, that I can make a dent in that are tree with nothin in pertikiler, only this fist full of bones, the alfired termination of my arm ; only I han't got nobody to stand me ;   and I han't going tu du it for nothin', no how it can be fixed.   I fags ! speakin' of the devil, here he comes.   Here comes a critter that may have a sneakin' notion arter losin' somethin'."

The person referred to by Seth came slowly up one of the narrow paths and entered the broad one in which Seth was standing.   The stranger's eyes were bent upon the ground, and he evidently did not see Seth.   He started when spoken to, and quickened his pace, as if he would gladly avoid encountering any one.

"Hulloo !   I say, stranger ! hold on a bit ; tu words in your ear."

The stranger turned back and looked hard at Seth ; Seth looked hard back again at the stranger for the space of about five seconds ; then rubbed his eyes ; crouched his body ; clapped both hands on either knee, and looked again.

"Du you know me, stranger ?" asked Seth.

"I do not, sir."

"By swear ; if I don't think you're the pertikilar feller that tuk it so allfired tu heart cause I smoked on the stage coach."

"Suppose I am, sir ; and what then ?"

"Oh, nothin', nothin', only I'm darned glad to see ye.   How are ye ?"

Seth extended his hand to the Englishman, but the Englishman thought proper to take no notice of it.

"Have you any business with me, sir ?" he asked, in the same cold tone and repulsive manner that he exhibited on the stage coach.

"I calkelate I have ; somethin' very partikular, tu."

"Be brief, then."

"If it don't in any way, either moral, religious, naterrally or unnaterrally perti-kilarly interfere with your pertikilar politics, I should jest like tu know your name."

"Pshaw ! if you have no other business——"

"Ye-a-s I have a little other business, now I knows your name ; and it's allfired pertikular kind of business, tu. I should jest like tu know, Mr. Shaw, what business you have in these ere grounds ?—that's all."

"Business !"

"Yes, business !" echoed Seth, his dandriff getting up a little. "Madam Jerome gave me pertikilar permission to wallop every uncivil feller what I caught in here."

"Do you belong to the asylum ?" asked the Englishman, his manner towards Seth suddenly changing.

"Do I belong to this ere asylum ? In course I do."

"How long have you been here ?"

"Oh, for that matter, a great length of time. Gwoin' on now for four days," he said to himself.

"Then perhaps you can give me the information I require ?"

"Nothin' more likely. I allus keeps my eyes open ; and besides, I has a perti-kilar kind of way by which I most pertikilarly find out all the pertikilar kind of business, pertikilar kinds of folks pertikelarly desire to keep pertikilarly tu 'em-selves. I has just gin you a pertikelar touch out. Oh, you are a sly one, but I found out your name at last, though."

"You can tell me who this Madame Jerome is ?"

"Ye-a-s, I calkelate I can," and Seth looked thoughtfully, and stroked his chin.

"You can tell me where she came from ?"

"Ye-a-s."

"How long she has been here ?"

"To a day."

"If there is a man who visits her ? How often he comes, or whether he stays all the time, how old he is, how he looks, whether tall or short, light or dark-complexioned, man or devil ? Tell me, good sir, tell me all ; tell me quick, or I shall go mad ! I am on the rack till I know if it be she."

All of these questions were put in rapid succession, and the Englishman who at first appeared so cold and repulsive, now grasped Seth tightly by the arm, and to all appearances was a raging maniac.

Seth at first intended to lead the Englishman on with the false hope that he could give him all the information he required, when, in fact, he was as profoundly ignorant upon all those points as the Englishman himself, and then he would leave him at last unsatisfied ; and so get his revenge on him for not revealing his name. But in the end, Seth began to think it wasn't quite so pleasant ; and that the Englishman had, indeed, gone stark mad.

"Why do you hesitate?" shrieked the Englishman, tightening his hold upon Seth's arm. "Tell me who this woman is ! keep me not in suspense, now that I have waited so many years ! tell me, tell me ! I implore you !"

"Why, I would, but you see——"

"But what?"

"The fact is—that is to say—I don't know."

Seth made a last effort, broke from the Englishman, and rushed up the avenue towards the asylum.

The Englishman, overcome by his feelings, sank upon a seat near by, and covered his face with his hands. When he looked up again, his face bore the same cold, stern look that marked it ever before.

"I was wrong to allow myself to be so moved," he said. "I will be more guarded in the future. But this woman—she has changed wonderfully in sixteen years, if it indeed be she. It must be she ! for she knew me, when I caught her eye, and fainted. After sixteen years of constant search, to find her here, in this secluded spot. A fit place it is, for such as she ! And that villain Savile, too !

would I knew if he be here! I would have rushed to the asylum at once, and confirmed my worst suspicions, but that I feared that he would escape me. He shall not escape me—for four days have I watched in vain for him! I have seen no one but this Yankee fool, and a young girl that daily comes with a book to read, by the chapel. I did not dare to question her, for she was at the theatre when she fainted. A few more days of patient watching, and I will be satisfied.

When Seth broke from the Englishman he rushed up the avenue, nor stopped till he reached the lawn in front of the asylum. Then he considered. 'At heart Seth was as tender as a woman. He felt he had injured the Englishman, and that he owed him some slight amends; so wheeling right-about, he went back. The Englishman was nowhere to be seen.

CHAPTER VIII.

THE ORPHANS AT SUPPER.

"How beautiful is sorrow, when 'tis drest
    By virgin innocence!   It makes
    Felicity in others seem deformed."

WHILE Annie was yet weeping, the bitter tears of insulted modesty and disappointed love—for the reader will have seen, ere this, that Erwin had made a deep impression on her heart, and that since the night when she accompanied Madame Jerome to the theatre, she had dwelt wholly upon his image, which accounts, though she did not perceive it, for the change in her feelings towards Charles McIver.

The reader will have seen, likewise, that the letter addressed her by Slickham, she attributed to Erwin, which was natural enough, as she did not see Slickham, neither did she know Erwin by his name. And from the fact that Slickham wrote that he saw her first at the theatre, she never dreamed he could be any other than the handsome stranger, who regarded her with so much of admiration in his looks.

But though she had thought of but little else save him since that evening, she was now determined to think of him no more. Poor girl! she little knew that to determine so, was but to think the more.

"She never could love a man possessed of such a mind," she thought, "nor marry one so vain and arrogant, as the author of the letter she had just received."

To come to this determination cost her many tears, indeed; and when the bell rang to call her to tea, her eyes were still red with weeping. But as every one in the asylum was expected regularly at her meals, she bathed her eyes in cold water, and hastened to the eating-room.

To her surprise Madame Jerome was at her usual place at the head of e table. She had not left her room since the night of her visit to the theatre, and ever since she had appeared much agitated. But now she appeared quite herself again.

Madame Jerome was never so happy as when surrounded by the little objects of her bounty. It is good to receive; but, oh, how much better to give. How the heart swells when extending the liberal hand—when the free heart opens its plentiful store, how the whole soul of liberality thrills with happiness, in witnessing the lighting up of joy in the lank face of want.

And that benevolent woman, surrounded by those little orphans, receiving their all from her, must feel—in proportion as finite compares with infinite—the extatic bliss of God, overlooking the children of men, drawing all they enjoy from his eternal bosom.

When supper was over, Madame Jerome requested Annie to follow her to her room.

"You must have noticed, my child," began Madame Jerome, when nicely seated in her comfortable arm chair, and Annie on a stool at her feet. "You must have noticed, that though I feel towards all the poor children under my charge, most kindly, that I hold thee in special favour?"

"You have indeed been most kind, dear, dear mother," said the grateful girl, taking the hand of Madame Jerome between her own. "Not only have you supplied my wants as soon as asked, but you have anticipated my very wishes. You have been to me all a dear mother could have been."

"It was, perhaps, because I took thee a helpless infant from your mother's arms, the very hour she bid farewell to this world for ever,—with the solemn promise that I would provide for you as an only child."

"You saw my mother then, before she died?" said Annie, her voice choked with her feelings. "I would give much to have seen her; and yet I have not missed her tender care. She could not have done more, or been more kind than you have been, my dear mother."

"It has been a pleasure to do for thee, my child; but enough of this. I did not intend to have got upon this theme when I called you to my room. I have something to tell you that I know will give you pleasure. In the first place, I must tell you, that in buying these lands and building this asylum, it cost me much more than I at first anticipated. Still I had considerable remaining money, which I put at interest, hoping the income would be sufficient to meet all the expenses o the establishment. In this I was disappointed. At first it was all sufficient; and I was able each year, to add some small portion of the interest to the principal. But for these last six years of the sixteen I have been here, my little charges have doubled on me; and I have in many instances, been obliged to deprive them of many comforts I would gladly have given them. You will be glad to hear that I have to-day received a donation, which will enable me to meet all the expenses of the establishment, amply, though I should have double the number I have at present."

"It is indeed good news."

"I will read you his letter."

Madame Jerome went to the table, and opening a small box, took from it a note.

"It is very flattering, and gives me more credit than is my due; but you shall hear it."

"Dear Madam.—In the few years I have lived, I have noted this fact. Those who possess the greatest amount of means to do good are the least ready to employ it for that end.

"What does this prove, but that the possession of such wealth monopolises every thought of its possessor? It does not follow that the rich man possesses not originally a good heart; but rather to keep what he hath, taxes every faculty, every thought which otherwise might be called off by the claims of the poor. And indeed, if occasionally some poor famishing woman stretches forth her hand to him for charity, asking bread for her starving children—is not his table spread with every dainty, and without a thought of his? he cannot understand why others' tables should not equally flow with milk and honey. Having no time to attend to the wants of others, or not fully understanding the nature of those wants, are the only excuses I can frame for that rich man, who refuses to give some portion of that wealth to the poor, which Providence has suffered him to acquire.

"But madam, for the sake of humanity and our common nature, I am happy to learn that there are some noble exceptions to the general rule, that a selfish heart close-fisted avarice and riches, bear each other company, and that there are some who feel that they are but the appointed stewards to dispense the abundance that Providence has provided them with.

"Of this class, madam, you have been pointed out to me as a shining member· I have made many inquiries (pardon me,) with regard to your treatment of the little ones under your protection—means you employ for their amusement—your manner of education, &c., &c., and in all there is wisdom, added to a hearty desire good and benefit our kind.

"And madam, permit me to say, that woman is infinitely better calculated for this work of benevolence than man. You have less to employ your mind, and consequently can better feel and understand others' wants than we—you have patience, discretion, and a warm sympathy, which we have not—your finer feelings enable you to understand, and give with that respect for the feelings of the recipient, so that while you give to the support of the body, you may not plant a thorn in its heart.

"For these reasons, madam, and believing as I do, that in your sphere you can better employ a portion of the wealth I have to spare, than I can in mine—I have sent you herewith enclosed a check of fifty thousand dollars, which please accept.

"With respect, I am, dear madam, Your obedient servant,

"PHILIP ERWIN."

"P.S. May I ask, without presuming too much upon your courtesy, permission to visit your benevolent institution? I shall be at leisure to-morrow afternoon, and shall be happy to avail myself of it, and pay my respects to one whose name the world mentions only with love and respect.

Tremont House, Boston, June, 18—.   "P. E."

When Madame Jerome had finished reading the letter, she laid it upon the table, and waited a moment to hear what Annie would say, while Annie was comparing in her own mind this letter with the one she had received the same afternoon.

"If he were only possessed of such feelings," she thought, "if he were only so noble and generous ; but while one letter uttered the sentiments of a noble and elevated mind, the other spoke its author to be selfish and conceited, possessing a mind with soil too shallow for any noble plant to find room for growth."

"Well, my child, you do not express an opinion."

"It is a noble present," she said, without raising her eyes from the floor. "And shows that the donor truly appreciates your character and worth."

"He flatters me, indeed. But what ought I to do, child? I have made no ac·knowledgments as yet."

"Send Seth to him in the morning with a note, thanking him for his munificent present, and say you are happy he intends paying you a visit."

"It shall be as you advise, my child. But you look ill, Annie! Your cheeks are pale, your eyes red with weeping, I fear; is anything the matter?" asked Madame Jerome, confidently.

This allusion to her looks, and the kind tone of Madame Jerome's voice, whom she loved and respected as a mother, brought her tears afresh.

"Why Annie, dear," said the kind-hearted woman, taking her favourite's hand. "This is something new! Has anything gone amiss?"

Annie only sobbed the more.

"I have been too much by myself of late. I have been too selfish in not attending to your wants. What has disturbed the feelings of my child?"

Annie would not for the world that Madame Jerome should know the real cause of her feelings; feelings which she blamed herself for giving way to, and therefore she answered, and indeed with sincerity ;—

"How can I be happy, when I see my kind mother unhappy? When I see her day after day, a prey to feelings I cannot relieve."

"Dear child! think no more of me. I received a fright in the theatre which I could not easily shake off. It is all over now. Go to your room, Annie, and think no more of me."

Annie kissed the good lady's hand, and left the room.

"Dear child!" sighed Madame Jerome, when Annie had closed the door. "How she has entwined herself around my heart. Few mothers love their offspring as I love her. She will be eighteen on Thursday next; and on that day I must make known to her who her parents were. She has not felt their loss. It has been my constant study that she should not. I have endeavoured that she, and all the dear creatures under my charge should feel, that though God has taken away their naatural protectors, He does not desert them ; but raises up others to do and to feel, to love and protect."

The next morning after the scene we have last described, Philip Erwin was in his room. Freelove and Snooksby were there likewise.

"Well, Phil, what's the order of the day?" asked Snooksby, turning a chair round on one leg. "Shall it be a drive to Fresh Pond, or to Mystic? S—— has some capital wine.

"To horse, to horse, mount, let us away,
Shall it be for Fresh Pond or Mystic—say?"

"I am entirely at your disposal for the present, gentlemen ; go where you list this morning, so you don't lose me this afternoon."

"Bound on a private expedition, eh, Phil? That's unfortunate, very. I had flattered myself that I should have the honour of showing you the inside of S——'s wine cellar, this afternoon. Haven't you a notion that way, Freelove?"

"Why, to say truth, Erwin," said Freelove, with his characteristic good breeding, "this scheme was of my projecting. I have made a purchase recently of a span of blacks, charming fellows ; and as I am not so good a judge of horseflesh as my friend Snooksby, here, why——"

"He invited me to ride behind them."

"Do not let me detain you, gentlemen," said Erwin, "I am no judge of the animal."

"Your opinion would be agreeable, notwithstanding. And besides, I heard Helen express a desire to visit Fresh Pond ; and as a brother is poor company for a sister, I presumed upon our long standing acquaintance, and proposed to appropriate a few hours of your time to her amusement."

"I am sorry that business renders it entirely out of my power to oblige you this afternoon ; but if to-morrow ——"

"Oh! quite as well to-morrow, Mr. Erwin," said Freelove, who cared not a fig whether he went at all or not. He wished only to draw him into his sister's society as much as possible.

"Oh, hope deferred !" sighed Snooksby, "I never felt the force of those words till now."

"But," said Erwin, remembering what Snooksby had said of his engagement with Helen. "I fear I shall trespass by this arrangement."

"Explain yourself, Mr. Erwin."

Erwin cast a look at Snooksby, who truth to say, remembering the same thing, blushed exceedingly for a man of his effrontery, and in order to cover it up, so managed as to sit the chair—which he was twirling on one leg—down upon one of his very best corns. The accident allowed him to make up as many wry faces as he thought necessary to suit the occasion.

"I shall be very happy to show Miss Freelove every attention consistent with the prior claims of my friend," said Erwin, keeping his eyes upon Snooksby's face, half suspecting that there was no truth in the assertion made by him. "But, as I have been informed——"

"The fact is, Freelove," said Snooksby, plucking up a little, "as I was telling Erwin—that is, Phil—as I was about to say—I mean Freelove—I was saying —d—n it! how my corn aches !"

"What does this mean, gentlemen?" said Freelove, looking from one to the other.

Erwin suspecting still more that Snooksby had imposed upon him, determined to sift it out.

"I will tell you in a few words, Mr. Freelove," he said. "Mr. Snooksby informed me——"

"Yes, that is what I said, Freelove, to a fraction," interrupted Snooksby, "But still, I flatter myself, I am not altogether selfish. Though I did at first hope to secure all of Phil's leisure time to myself; yet if you desire it, and he prefers Helen's society to mine—why—I——"

Happily for Snooksby—for Erwin was fairly aroused and determined that Snooksby should not cover over such an assertion, where any lady was concerned, with such loose subterfuge—they were interrupted by voices outside the door in angry dispute.

"But I say I will go in."

"Not until I have announced you."

"I can do my own business, in my own pertikilar way. Stand out of my moonlshine or I'll grease ye, and pin back your ears and swaller yer down jest like a new aid egg."

A heavy hand was laid upon the door. It flew open.

"It isn't my fault; I couldn't help it!" began the waiter, apologizingly.

"Oh, you get out, now! nobody wont give you a peeling, seeing has now you did yer darndest to keep me out. So you might jest as well make yerself scarce."

The waiter disappeared, and Seth turned to the three gentlemen who had been so unceremoniously stopped in their unpleasant colloquy, and holding out his large bony hand to Erwin, said,—

"I am pisky glad to see ye well."

"Thank you," responded Erwin.

"Perhaps you don't know me?"

"I confess it."

"Du tell me! Some folks have a partikilarly short memory, but that's neither here nor there! I remember you jest as easy as nothin."

"I believe I am growing wiser!" said Erwin. "Is it Mr. Lyon?"

"I'm the very critter, Seth Lyon, and no mistake. You remember the little fracas on the stage, too, I calkerlate?"

"I do. Will you be seated?"

"Don't care if I du, as I've got some allfired pertikilar business tu du with you. I've got a letter from Madame Je——"

"Ah, yes! I remember—I will spare you the particulars, Mr. Lyon," said Erwin, who had his reason for keeping his donation to St. Mary from the knowledge of Freelove and Snooksby. "Gentlemen, I fear I shall disturb you with this little business I have on my hands."

"Oh, not in the least, Phil! I beg you won't mind us, my dear boy!" said Snooksby, having recovered somewhat from the effect of dropping the chair upon his foot.

"But Madame Je——"

"Yes, I know what you would say, Mr. Lyon! Gentlemen, I bid you good morning."

"We will not detain you now, Mr. Erwin," said Freelove. "I shall see you to morow.'

"If you have so arranged it."

"You are too particular, Phil, you are decidedly. This fellow wouldn't disturb us in the least. But as you are so determined,—till to morrow be it."

The two young worthies left the room. "Contemptible puppies," muttered Erwin, when they had gone out; and then turned to Seth. "You are in Madame Jerome's employ, then?"

"I rather calkerlate I am. You see I went tu see uncle Joel, as I told you I was going in; an if you'll believe it, he was so alfired nice a-weighing out his fish with his fine clothes on, he wouldn't speak to a feller. That was a little bit more no

New Hampshire grit could stand, so I streaked it out of the store without sayin, nothin.' The next day I went to see the intelligence man, and he said it was the best way as I wan't known in these parts, to put a piece in the paper 'bout me ; and sure enough the next day I had a letter from Madame Jerome. The intelligence man said if I was pertikilar about having a pertikilar kind of place, I had better nab it at once. So I went right off, and let myself. But how do you get along ?'

"I have not been quite so fortunate in obtaining a place, as you," said Erwin, who had meantime opened and read Madame Jerome's most excellent note.

SETH LYON'S UNCEREMONIOUS ENTRY.—SEE PAGE 32.

Seth eyed the letter as if he suspected it had something to do with him or his place.

"Are you arter a place out there, tu ?" he asked.

"No," answered Erwin, smiling, "I shall in no way injure your prospecst. This note is upon other business."

This answer seemed to satisfy Seth, and after a half hour spent in asking all sorts of questions, he took his leave.

No. 5.

CHAPTER IX.

THE SURPRISE.

"White as a white sail on a dusky sea,
When half the horizon's clouded and half free,
Fluttering between the dim wave and the sky,
Is hope's last gleam in man's extremity."

THE afternoon was bright and clear, the air soft and balmy. The little girls of St. Mary had put on their gayest apparel, and the young maidens donned their white frocks and happy smiles. Every thing wore a glad appearance. Madame Jerome looked younger by ten years; and even Annie, in the general excitement, half forgot her sad heart, and looked happy again.

Ever since his return from the city, Seth had vainly guessed at the cause of preparation; had asked every miss he dared to address, "what on arth was on foot," but they, being as ignorant as himself, of course could give him no satisfactory information. It was hinted, however, and reached Seth's ears, that a great man was coming to visit the asylum.

Things were in this train, when, about four o"clock, a hackney coach drew up at the gate of the principal avenue leading to St. Mary. A young man got out, and after giving some directions to the driver, entered the grounds.

He had never been there before, and as he passed up the gravelled walk, he stopped to witness everything of interest that attracted his notice. On arriving at the verge of the wood, the green lawn broke upon his sight, peopled with a hundred little girls and maidens. Happy creatures! Some were driving their hoops; others chasing one another in childish glee, while the older and more sedate looked on and enjoyed the wild delight of the younger.

But little time, however, was allowed the stranger to enjoy the innocent and happy scene, for Seth's ever watchful eyes fell on his figure, and he hastened down to learn his pleasure.

"So, it aint you, though, is it?" he exclaimed, holding out his hand as he drew near. "Who on arth thought o' seein' you here at this pertikilar time, Mr Erwin?"

"There is nothing very surprising in it, is there, my friend?"

"No, nothin', only I'm pertikilarly glad to see you, cause we are gwoin' to have a great time here in a few minnits. Madame Jerome expects a great man here—General Jackson, mebby—this arternoon, to see her little human critters, what she stuffs with all sorts of knowledge and other food; but you can come up all the same; though she's an all fired great lady, she don't feel above nobody."

"Is she so very affable?"

"The most pertikilar kind of affable. She treats the little critters for all the world as if she was marm to the hull lot. And then there's Miss Annie—he lets her go round with her, and treats her just like an only child."   "

"She uses partiality, then."

"Not by four chalks. Miss Annie is a pertikilar kind of critter, and deserves pertikilar kind of attention. Then she is older than the others, and looks arter the little ones, and hears them say their A B C's; and besides, everybody loves her. Mister Charles says, if she isn't a human angel. then there never was one."

"Does Mr. Charles belong to the asylum?"

"Not zackly, though he comes here most every day, and sits way out there in the woods, and tries to get a peep at Miss Annie, poor thing! He isn't long for this terrestrial world; his face is as pale as nothin' at all."

While Seth was yet enumerating the "pertikilar" virtues of Madame Jerome, Annie, and Charles, he heard a carriage rapidly approaching up the road; and, thinking it might contain the illustrious individual who was to honour them with a call, he drew Erwin towards the asylum.

"Come," he said, "I rather calkilate the great critter's comin'. We'll go up into my room, and have a good stare at him when he comes up the road, free gratis for nothin'."

Madame Jerome saw Erwin from the window approaching the asylum, and though he was younger than she had supposed, yet his noble look and manly bearing at once convinced her that he was the person expected, and she hastened to the door to meet him.

As she made her appearance at the door, Seth pressed forward to introduce his friend, for, to say truth, he was not a little proud of his acquaintanceship, seeing that he was a noble specimen of a man, and wore exceeding fine cloth.

"This is Mr. Erwin, marm," he said, making a decided good hit at a bow; "a pertikilar friend of mine, what I have been acquainted with for ———"

Seth was here stopped in the middle of his speech following the presentation by Mrs. Jerome's kindly offering Erwin her hand, and warmly welcoming him to St. Mary.

Seth was left standing on the steps, staring after their receding figures, not a little puzzled at what he saw; and when they had disappeared from his sight, he hinted that there might be more in it, arter all, than he know'd on.

Madame Jerome conducted her guest into a large, well-furnished room, the windows of which looked out upon the lawn, and commanded a full view of the happy little fraternity. Madame Jerome, calling a servant, sent to desire Annie to come down, who was still in her own room.

"It has been my determination," said Madame Jerome, " to take my children with me out into the world as fast as they arrive at a sufficient age. We are retired here, as you see, sir; few seek us out; and the young maidens, brought up in this secluded place, can be told, but cannot comprehend, the many wiles and snares that they are liable to encounter. Like young birds, they should plume their wings, and by short flights learn confidence, and strengthen themselves to encounter the journey of life."

"Such a view of their wants is worthy of yourself. Have many left you?"

"Not one, as yet; and inded I have but one of sufficient age to present to the world. I take every opportunity to prepare her for the change that must soon take place. I have sent for her but now; she will soon be here."

While Madame Jerome was yet speaking, the door opened, and Annie entered the room. Madame Jerome rose to meet her.

"Annie, my dear, this is Mr. Erwin," she said, leading Annie forward.

Annie raised her eyes to Erwin's face, essayed to speak, but could not. The blood rushed to her heart; the colour left her cheek, her frame trembled, and she would have sunk to the floor but for the support of Madame Jerome.

As the reader knows, Annie saw in Erwin the stranger that came to Madame Jerome's assistance, in company with Snooksby, at the theatre; the one that had filled her thoughts ever since; and the supposed author of the insulting letter she received afterwards. She was undeceived now, and he stood before her all shs could hope or wish. But the knowledge proved almost too much for her. Sudden joy is quite as overpowering as grief.

Erwin saw the sudden change in Annie, and attributing it to any rather than the right cause, was also embarrassed, and turned away and looked from the window.

The young girls were still at play upon the lawn, and their wild shouts rang out right merrily. Erwin watched their free and agile movements for a while, and then turned to Madame Jerome, who had seated herself—Annie by her side, her eyes bent upon the ground—and said,—

"To be the author of so much joy and happiness in these little ones, must be bliss enough for this world. To look out from this window and witness this exhibition of childish sports, listen to their merry laugh, like the caroling of a hundred swallows upon their holiday gathering—their hearts as light as the wild bird upon the wing—and to know yourself to be the creator of this heaven surely must be an abundant reward."

"It is, indeed. Few can know the delights flowing from such a loving and obedient family as I am surrounded with, unless, like me, they learn from experience."

Madame Jerome turned to Annie, and seeing she was pale and excited, and sat musing in her chair, said,—

"I fear you are not well, my child; you had better return to your chamber."

Annie felt grateful for an excuse to retire, and rose to leave the room.

"I do indeed feel ill," she said.

"Does Miss Annie suffer from exposure at the theatre?" ventured Erwin.

"Not in the least, sir."

As Annie answered, she raised her eyes to his, and meeting his steady yet respectful gaze, they quickly sought the ground again, and her face, before so pale, assumed the carnation's hue.

"Mother has not been able to leave her room since till yesterday."

"Was it you that—that—helped us to our carriage?"

"It was. I regret, exceedingly, that you have been indisposed in consequence."

"It was slight, sir. Annie, we will excuse you, child," said madame, wishing to change the conversation.

Annie gladly sought her chamber again. The feelings that the unexpected meeting with Erwin gave rise to, were of a character only to be indulged in solitude, where no eye save that of the searcher of hearts was upon her. There we will leave her.

It will not interest the reader, perhaps, though to Erwin it was a feast to the moral being—so to speak—to follow them through the different rooms and departments of St. Mary. Therefore we will pass over it.

Erwin took his leave of Madame Jerome about six o'clock. On his way home he was racked with contending emotions. He loved the beautiful Annie with his whole soul. He felt, from the moment he first saw her, that their destinies were inseparably connected; and as it was so, he was miserable.

He felt she could not love him; her strange actions when they met, seemed to say so. He did not expect her to love him, indeed; but there was something in her manner that led him to believe she did not feel towards him that indifference, even, he might expect, as a stranger. Did she love Charles, spoken of by Seth? He said Charles loved her, and what woman's heart can witness the constant devotion of a loving soul, and not at last send out some tendril blossom to meet it in sympathy?

"And why should I desire her love?" he thought. "We can never be united. My vow to a dying father must be accomplished. He little thought it would entail such misery upon me; he never dreamed that it could be thus repulsive to my feelings, or he never would have made the request. It matters little now. It is past; I have given my word, and must redeem it. My only hope is that she will refuse me; and then, if I cannot obtain the love of Annie, at least I shall ot sin in loving her."

CHAPTER X.

THE PLOT.

"My poverty, but not my will, consents."

"I pay thy poverty, and not thy will."

"Put this in any liquid thing you will,
And drink it off; and, if you have the strength
Of twenty men, it would despatch you straight."

"There is thy gold; worse poison to men's souls,
Doing more murders in this loathsome world,
Than these poor compounds that thou may'st not sell :
I sell thee poison, thou hast sold me none.
Farewell; buy food, and get thyself in flesh,"

NOTWITHSTANDING Erwin took his way back to the city in no enviable state of mind, leaving behind him one equally unhappy with himself—for although she loved Erwin with all the strength of a first attachment, she never dreamed he loved, or could love her in return—the sun went down as bright as usual, the moon rode abroad with a bright cheerful countenance, and the stars came out as thickly as when the world was two thousand years younger, making the tranquil night nearly as light as noon-day.

It might have been nine o'clock, when the figure of a man stepped from the shadow of the wood upon the lawn in front of St. Mary. His figure was slight and bowed, his face pale and sorrowing, and his whole appearance bespoke him suffering in body, as well as mind.

He stood a few minutes with his face towards that part of the heavens where the moon was holding her court, as if holding silent communion with some being upon her bright surface.

"Months, years hence," at length he said, "in some distant land, I shall look upon that bright orb, and fancy it still looks down upon this asylum and lawn and wood that sleep so tranquilly now, with the same smiling face she hath to-night. Oh! how I shall love thee, silver moon! for thou wilt be the same as thou art now. Thou wilt not change with distance! thy serene face will greet me as an old familiar friend, when all else is strange around, and stranger eyes alone look into mine. Yet I shall envy thee, fair queen; for thou, from thy high throne, canst look upon this loved spot of earth, canst watch (glorious privilege), when slumbers veil *her* eyes in sleep! and perchance she, on such a night as this, may look upon thee as I do now; and then shall thy bright face grow brighter from the reflection of her own ; and watching, I shall see the change, which shall be to me a token."

Then lowering his eyes, he seemed to be taking leave of the wood and lawn, and every familiar object ; and then with a slow step he crossed the lawn, and approached the asylum. He had taken but a few steps, when a man crossed his path, looking him steadily in the face for a moment, and then passed on, and entered the wood. This appeared somewhat strange to the person that had but now given utterance to his unhappy thought, but he passed on, and tapped on a window at the back of the asylum, when the voice of Seth Lyon cried out, "Who's there ?" at the same time he threw up the window.

"Are you dressed ?"

"Oh, it's you, Mister Charles. Why—I'm not wholly pertikilarly dressed; I've got my trousers and jacket on—why ?"

"Will you do me the favour to request Annie, in my name, to come to the little chapel. I have something of importance to say to her."

"Can't you wait till mornin' ? she may be tu bed."

"Not well ; and yet I know not if I ought to disturb her."

Charles turned as if to leave, when the moon's beams fell on his face, and Seth saw that it was unusually pale and agitated. He called him back.

"Then it's for somethin' pertikilar?" he said. "I don't much mind running up to see if I can raise her."

"You will oblige me by doing so, if it is not too much trouble to you."

"Why, as for that matter, I don't much mind a little trouble, if it's only for anythin' in partikilar. But you see, I have to be a little pertikilar myself, bein' as I am, kind of overseer here. But I rather calkerlate I can trust you, any how."

Saying which, Seth closed the window. "Now, I've a great notion tu know what's going on," soliloquised Seth, giving the last stroke to his toilet. "The critter don't want her for nothin', that's clear as preachin'. I'll jest du the business to her, and then I'll sneak round, and see what's goin' on."

While Charles found his way back to the place of assignation, we will call the reader's attention to another scene, enacting near at hand.

Within the shadow of a tree, standing by the gate to the main entrance, leading to St. Mary, stood a man. By his dress, it might be supposed he had just left a ball-room ; and by his trembling, one would think he was suffering under an attack of the ague.

"I wish that fellow would come along," at length he said. "It is dem disagreeable to be kept waiting here at this time of the night in these woods, it is, by my faith. There may be bears here. How that charming creature can live in this horrid place, I can't divine, I can't, by my faith ; it's shocking to think of it." And the valiant gentleman leaned against the tree to steady his overtaxed nerves. "I'll not stay here much longer for all the angels in Christendom, I won't, by my faith. It is now full five minutes past the time when Freelove promised the fellow should be here. I am half inclined to change my mind, and go back to the city, I am, by my faith."

Just then, a man, dressed in a long surtout and broad-brimmed slouched hat, that entirely shaded his face, entered the avenue from the road. As the moon shone full upon the new comer, the whole person was distinctly seen by the gentleman in the hadow of the tree ; but he did not dare to venture out until he saw the man in the surtout stop, and slowly place both hands upon his breast. By this signal agreed upon, he knew it to be the man that was to meet him, and he left his concealment.

"Mr. Slickham?" asked the man in the slouched hat.

"My name, most unequivocally ; and yours?"

"Is no concern of thine. I was sent here by a Mr. Freelove to do your bidding. I am come ; if you have anything to do, name it."

"Mr. Freelove doubtless acquainted you with my intentions?"

"He told me that you wished to carry off a girl; that——"

"Yes, I understand. But you will please to modulate your tone to the occasion. We may be overheard, which would be dem disagreeable ; it would, by my faith."

The man reproved looked suspiciously about him, and then pulled his hat still further over his eyes, as if he feared detection as much as his companion.

"Well, what do you propose?" asked Slickham, with a little more nerve, now that he was no longer alone.

"Firstly,—that you give me a sweetener of a hundred dollars ; secondly——"

"Very modest, by dem! a hundred dollars for carrying off a girl? You are exorbitant ; you are, by my faith."

"Consider the work I have done, and am to do ; the risk I run of detection. In the first place, I have spent one night in learning where the beauty lays her delicate head ; and now I am to entice her out, and convey her to the carriage you have in waiting, and for ever hold my peace afterwards. Now, if for all this you are not willing to pay me a hundred dollars, why, you may go further and fare worse."

The man in the slouched hat made a movement to leave the ground.

" Upon second thoughts, it is little enough; it is, by my faith," said Slickham, staying his companion. " We are agreed; so now——"

" Cash down."

" Will you not trust me?"

" Catch one rogue to trust another."

" Do you call me a rogue? You are impertinent; you are, by my faith."

" Why it smells a little of roguery, I should think; to force a young lady from her home against her will."

" I will give her a better one; I will, by my faith."

" It matters little to me what you do with her; but if you are to enjoy a pretty woman through my instrumentality, you must pay for it. I'll have a hundred dollars before I move in this affair."

" I havn't got so much money with me; true, by dem."

" That we can manage."

The man in the slouched hat produced a small slip of paper from the ample pocket of his surtout, and handed it to Slickham,

" You deposite at the Merchants' Bank, I believe."

" I do; but how should you know it, I can't well tell; I can't by my faith."

" There is a check for one hundred dollars; put your name to that, and then we will proceed. Here are pen and ink. You see I am prepared."

Slickham examined the check by the light of the moon, and finding it correct, signified his willingness to sign it."

" Use your hat for a writing-desk," said he of the slouched hat; " you cannot use mine."

Crouching upon the ground, he placed the pen in Slickham's hand. Slickham was about to sign, when the stranger started to his feet, exclaiming,—" listen?" and while Slickham was thrown off his guard, quick as thought he swallowed the unsigned check, and supplied its place with another.

" I thought I heard some one approaching," he said, still listening, and peering into the wood. " I might have been mistaken. It would not be healthy for any one, to let me catch them skulking about."

Thus saying' he crouched upon the ground, again, and held the check upon the hat for Slickham to sign. Slickham listened for a moment, and hearing nothing to alarm him, hurriedly affixed his name to the paper.

The stranger carefully put away the check, and then bidding Slickham follow him, entered the grove on the left.

Seth, when he had made known Charles's request to Annie, determined to learn what the pale young gentleman wanted, took a circuitous route for the place of assignation.

Annie immediately tied on her cape bonnet and left the room. She picked a rose as she passed through the garden, and placed it in her bosom. Lightly she tripped along the lawn, innocently wondering the while, what Charles could want of her at this late hour of the night. Without fear, she entered the grove.

She had not proceeded far when a voice caused her to stop, and a man entered the path a few feet in advance of her.

" Is it you, Charles?"

The man made no reply, but immediately seized her round the waist. A shriek broke from the terrified girl, and she struggled to disengage herself from the firm grasp of her captor.

" Confusion!" muttered the man, covering her mouth with his hand to silence her cries. " Quick, quick! Slickham! lay hold and force her along!"

" I?—I can't think of it! I never lay violent hands on a lady; I don't, by my faith. I paid you for doing that."

" Fool! don't you see I can use but one hand? This is no time for trifling! Her cries may have reached St. Mary; and in ten minutes we shall have hell about our ears in the shape of an old woman and a hundred little brawling brats. Lay hold of her feet, and help carry her along."

While Slickham was deciding how to act, Charles, who had heard the cries of

Annie, came rushing up the path; and at once divined the cause of alarm. He was no longer weak—his frame became instantly strong, and his nerves twice their former strength ; and without fearing the result, or reckoning the odds against him, rushed upon the enemy,

Slickham was the first in his way.   With one spring at his collar, he laid him over his foot on his face in the path.   The stranger, who held the now fainting Annie, was not so easily overcome.   He was apparently much stronger than Charles, besides his fair burden, in some degree, shielded him ; for Charles scarcely dared to attack for fear he should do her some harm.   He did not reflect long, however, but gave the stranger a blow in the face that sent him reeling backward, and caused him to lose his hold of the unconscious girl, whom Charles received in his arms.

The stranger sprang to his feet, and smarting from the blow he had received, prepared himself to pay it back with interest.   At the same moment he was caught from behind ; and turning, he encountered the stern gaze, and bold and determined front of a man quite his equal.   Seeing he was matched, and more, the stranger in the slouched hat sprang from the path, and in an instant was out of sight in the wood.

Slickham, whom Charles had so unceremoniously made to kiss the ground, had his nose skinned its entire length.   He got upon his feet again, and without waiting to gather up the pieces of his torn proboscis, was making for his carriage, when he was gently requested to stop.   Seth had likewise heard the cries of Annie, and stood before him.

" Jest hold on a bit, stranger ; if ye ain't in no pertikilar hurry," he said, laying his hand on Slickham's collar.   " Mebby you an't pertikilar which way you go, and 'll take a few steps with me."

" Where do you take me to ?" cried Slickham in alarm, finding himself hurried along the path, in spite of all his efforts to the contrary.

" Only tu a short walk for yer health.   If I walks faster than suits your pertikilar convenience, just speak and tell us on't."

" Your actions are really shocking ; they are, by my faith."

" Oh, don't be skeared too much ; for we've jest got tu the end on't."

Just then they arrived at the pond before mentioned. which now lay like a sheet of polished silver, reflecting a thousand mimic worlds from its bosom.

" Surely, you don't intend——"

" Yes I du, though ; if it's only to wash the blood off your face."

" I won't trouble you; I won't by my faith."

" Oh, it's no sort of trouble; I shall pertikilarly like it ; and I rather calkerlate a cold bath will du you good.   How should you like to be ducked; feet or head first."

Seth drew Slickham towards the water.

" You cannot be serious in what you say ; by my faith, you can't," said Slickham, holding back.   " Surely you can't intend to carry your threats into execution ?"

" Can't I though ! You'll pretty directly find out what I du mean, I calkerlate."

" Mercy, Mercy !"

" Oh get out now ! Don't open your mouth so wide; you'll skear the little fishes."

Slickham clung to Seth, with the despair of a drowning man ; but the superior strength of the latter enabled him to free himself with ease, and raising the unfortunate Slickham from the ground, and amid cries and supplications, he plunged him unceremoniously into the pond.   The water was not deep, however, and with two or three quick drawn breaths, the unfortunate man gained his feet, and made for the shore, accompanied with the entreaties of Seth that he would not wet his feet, or he might take cold.

Scarcely had the man in the slouched hat disappeared, when the stranger that came to Charles's assistance (whom Seth would have recognised as the Englishman) disappeared also, and before Charles could thank him for his timely aid.

Left alone, with her he loved above all else in his arms—her face lying close to his own—her warm breath upon his cheek—for a few moments he was blessed.

How throbbed his heart against hers; how, by the pale beams of the moon, struggling through the foliage above them, he watched each change in that dear face, as the blood came slowly back to her heart.

"Shall I take one fond kiss?" he said; "one parting kiss, that shall prove a *souvenir* for the long years I am away? It is the first I ever dared to hope for; it will be the last that the fates will give me. 'Tis no sacrilege; no passion gives

FREELOVE PRESENTS THE CHECK TO NED BARNABEE.—See page 43.

birth to the desire. It is the seal of tried friendship—the last breath of hope. Soft! that kiss, like a charm, gives free current to the blood, and her cheek glows with returning life. How do you feel now, Annie?"

"Is it you, Charles? They told me you wished to see me, when ———." She closed her eyes again, as if to shut out remembrance.

"I know it all, Annie; but you are safe now, thanks to the assistance of a stranger. Here is Seth—you had better return with him to the asylum."

"I could not say farewell," said the unhappy Charles, when left alone; "the

No. 6.

word stuck in my throat. It is better as it is ; she will never know the anguish that wrings my heart. Father," he continued, sinking upon the ground, "be thou her shield in sorrow and distress ; soften and cheer her journey through this life ; and, when consistent with thy Providence, bring us together in thy home beyond the skies."

CHAPTER XI.

THE DISCOVERY.

"Thus doth the ever-changing course of things
Run a perpetual circle, ever turning;
And that same day that highest glory brings,
Brings us to the point of back returning."

THE city clocks were striking the hour of eleven, when one of the principal actors in the scene recorded in the last chapter (he of the surtout and slouched hat) crossed Cambridge-bridge, and took his way up Cambridge-street. Though late, the street still presented a lively appearance ; peopled with the fairest of the sex that Boston-hill afforded, and hundreds of the bearded gentry making themselves as agreeable as circumstances would allow.

The numerous drinking shops were also tenanted with a mixed population of male and female, and coarse oaths and wild laughter, more merry than musical, greeted him on every hand.

Drawing his hat close over his eyes, he passed on, nor stopped till he came to the foot of the little rise, now leading into Bowdoin-square, and entered a tap-room nicknamed "the Fly-trap," kept by one Ned Barnabee. This, like all others of the same class, found many a customer in the fairer portion of the children of men, and now was literally crammed with such and their lovers.

"Is Ned in ?" asked he in the slouched hat, hurriedly, of a youth in the bar, whose red face seemed to say that he took a little wine himself occasionally, for his stomach's sake.

"In his private room, I suppose."

"Ho, ho!" exclaimed a dark-eyed girl, making up to him, and laying hold of his arm, which drew the attention of all in the room. "Some jewels you wish to turn into cash, I suppose. Never mind, I will take them of you, and give you back your change in love, which will be more agreeable to you than Ned's sour looks, I take it."

The individual in the slouched hat made no reply, but shook off the girl, and passed on towards the door in the back of the room.

"Go ! you are as crabbed as old Ned himself," said the girl, angrily.

He opened the door, crossed a narrow entry, and entered a room beyond, as one familiar with the place.

An old man sat by a grate of smouldering Newcastle coal, and although it was midsummer, he was crouched close to the grate, which, truth to say, gave out more of smoke than heat. A small tin lamp, on an old table within his reach, gave a faint, flickering light, just sufficient to reveal his little fleshless person and bald crown, that shone like polished pine, in contrast with a frill of black hair encircling his head.

"Who are you? and what do you want ?" he asked, sharply, and without rising from the fire, hearing some one enter the room.

"My business is private—had we not better take the next room? We may be intruded upon here."

"Humph, private—everything is private now-a-days. All a secret—no honest dealings—everything must be done without witnesses."

The old man took the lamp from the table, and without once looking at the person who had broken in upon his scheming solitude, led the way into the adjoining room.

"Now, your business!"

"Give me the money on that check."

The old man took the check and held it up to the light.

"He, he! Tightlace Slickham's check for ten thousand dollars?"

The check and signature underwent a critical examination in the old man's hands, after which he turned his little searching eyes upon the stranger, the lower part of whose face alone was visible.

"Remove your hat, sir," said the old man, in an authoritative tone. "I deal with no man with his head under a bushel. I like honest, open dealing."

"Your habits and life declare as much," said the stranger, tauntingly. "Nevertheless, old Honesty, you shall have all the light you ask for."

Thus saying, the stranger removed his hat and threw it upon the floor.

"Mr. Freelove," said the old man, with more of respect in his tone.

"You see my face too often to forget it, I perceive; though it be somewhat disfigured with a black spot."

"How did your honour get it?"

"By being too fond of amusement. But come, it is getting late."

Barnabee brought down a chair for Freelove and another for himself.

"Will your honour be seated? What can I do for your honour?"

"Honour be d——d! Give me the money on that check you hold in your hand."

"Was there ever such assumption! To suppose that Ned Barnabee should have that enormous sum about him. You are wild, young man."

"This is idle talk. You know well enough you have twice the sum about you."

"Is the check good?"

"As any man's check in Boston. He has a large sum in the bank at all times."

"Why doesn't Mr. Freelove present the check himself?"

"You are a wise one, and must have the whole story, I see. Well, you shall have it. I do not fear to trust you, where there is anything to be made by keeping silent."

"Except it interfere with my notions of honest dealing."

"God save thy honesty! It is as capacious as the far-famed Banyan tree. Nothing of vice, but what may find shelter beneath its branches; nothing that bears the name of crime but may find a covert unseen; and, indeed, should the devil himself seek its shelter, it would take him in, cloven foot and all."

"You flatter me, truly."

"Say no more of your conscience, but let me have the money on that check."

"You forget, Mr. Freelove, you were to tell me how you came by it."

"And so I will. By chance I learned, no matter how, that Slickham, who, by the way, is a lecherous devil, had some designs on a young and virtuous female of my acquaintance, residing a few miles from the city. In a word, he had determined, knowing her to be unprotected, with the assistance of a hireling, to carry her off. Having some desire for adventure, and wishing to thwart him in his base designs, I procured this disguise and was upon the spot.

"We had a hard fight of it; but notwithstanding I had two to contend against, I came off conqueror and without a scratch, if I except the slight bruise here on my face. Slickham I secured, while his accomplice escaped. Oh, you should have seen the fellow plead when I had got him down. Ha, ha, ha! My surtout and slouched hat were formidable. But why should I recapitulate? Enough for you to know, that he gave me the check which you hold in your hand, to spare him, and keep the matter secret."

"If this be true ——"

"Dare you doubt it, sir?"

"I ask again, why not present the check and receive the money yourself?"

"Again, I say, you are wondrous wise. See you not Slickham knew not to whom he gave the check?"

"Well?"

"You might suppose I would gladly keep it from him still."

"What has this to do with ——"

"Just this. I am known to the Paying Teller at the Merchants' Bank, and should I present the check myself, I might in some way implicate myself in the affair."

"Did it never occur to you I run the same risk?"

"I cannot see it. In the first place, to-morrow at nine o'clock, you get the money, which will be of the greatest importance to you, I take it; and then afterwards, should Slickham kick up about it, which is not very likely, what will it amount to? The check is no forgery—the signature is genuine. And should it turn out that they should trace it back to you, you have only to say that you came honestly by it; that you took it of a stranger leaving the city before banking hours, and wanted the money."

Barnabee reflected a few moments, and then going to a chest of drawers, took from them a paper which also bore Slickham's signature, and compared them with each other. Being apparently satisfied that the signature was genuine, he returned the paper to the drawer and resumed his seat.

"Well, supposing—I say, supposing I should conclude to present the check, and should now give you the money on it, how much of it shall I retain for my service?"

"Now you come to points. Well, for this great service, which will cost you about as much labour as to turn out a three cent nipper for some drunken customer, I will give you fifty dollars."

Barnabee started to his feet and handed Freelove the check.

"It is getting to be late, Mr. Freelove; and I am an old man and require rest."

"I will not go till you cash this check."

"Will not?"

"No, will not."

"Am I to be robbed in my own house?"

"No, but I require your service, and will have it."

"You talk very loudly, Mr. Freelove."

"I care not; I have given you thousands for nothing. Now I wish for a slight favour, and have offered you fifty dollars in liquidation, you don't seem inclined to accept it. Now I will hear how much your conscience will allow you to take."

Barnabee sat down again.

"Why, I am willing to do what I can to accommodate; but you must see that I run a great risk of losing my money."

"Set the risk at the highest point, and then say how much must I give."

"Why if you feel inclined to give me——I shall not meet your views."

"Name it."

"Two thousand dollars would——"

"Two thousand furies!"

"It will be a handsome speculation for you, then; eight thousand dollars will do for one night's work."

"Old man! I am not to be trifled with. Do not think I will allow you to take advantage of my necessities. I want the money; you can help me to it without injury to yourself; and you shall, or——"

"It is idle for you to assume this high tone, Mr Freelove," said Barnabee, his eyes flashing indignantly. "I have not committed myself to you You are in my power, and——"

"Ah, do you threaten me, old man?" gasped Freelove, making up to Barnabee, with his hands clenched.

Barnabee stood his ground. His little eyes looked like two balls of fire; but in other respects he appeared calm and collected.

"You dare not lay a finger on me," he said, with a scarcely perceptible trembling of his voice.

"Not dare!"

"No! then you would get no money; and I take it you want some badly. Of the large sums I advanced you but a short time since, you haven't a dollar left, I suppose."

"Not a dollar."

"And you would do violence to the old man who has supplied your extravagant demands for more than a year, and who is still willing to advance more!"

"Yes," interrupted Freelove, bitterly, "and how have you supplied my extravagant demands? By taking two dollars in real estate for every dollar of money you advanced me. Is it not enough that you have my sister's whole patrimony and mine, valued at forty thousand dollars, for less than half that sum, but you must now filch from me two thousand more?"

"Why, as to your patrimony, you came to me and wanted money. I required security, and you gave it me. It was all a fair business transaction—honest dealing between man and man. Now you have a check on the Merchant's Bank drawn by one Tightlace Slickham, which you say is good. It may or it may not be; of that I run the risk. I offer you eight thousand dollars, and take the paper. If you will take it, you have but to say so, and I place the money in your hands; if you will not, you can carry it to another market."

"Is that the most you will give me?" he asked, with an effort to appear calm.

"The utmost farthing."

"Give me the money."

Barnabee again examined the check, as if he thought there still might be some deception; but being again satisfied, he said,—

"Wait in the next room; I will bring the money to you."

"Are you afraid that I shall learn the way to your hoard?"

"You can as well wait in the next room as here. I will not keep you long."

"I have as good cause to mistrust you, as you have to mistrust me. I will hold the check, if you please, till I see the money."

"Oh, as you will."

Taking the check, Freelove withdrew to the next room, where he had first found Barnabee crouched over the grate. The room was now in total darkness; and feeling his way along, he seated himself in the chair usually occupied by the old miser himself. He had been seated scarcely a minute, when he heard the door leading from the tap-room open and some one enter.

"Why don't you have a light, Mr. Barnabee?" said a small voice.

Freelove knew the voice belonged to some person (whoever it might be) who expected to find old Ned in his usual place; and he knew, too, that he could easily pass himself off for that worthy personage, without fear of detection.

"Your lamp has gone out," ventured the same voice.

"Who are you, that comes to disturb me at this time of night?" growled Freelove, assuming, as well as he could the angry tone of Barnabee.

"I am Mary, confidential maid to the young lady on Mount Vernon-street, sir. She bade me come late, for fear I should meet some one who would know me, sir."

"So this old fool has to do with pretty ladies, does he?" thought Freelove.

"You did well to come late; as she said, you might have met with some one. Well, what does she want now."

"She bade me give you this letter, sir."

Freelove hurriedly took the note, and at the same time slipped a small piece of money into the girl's hand. He gave her a very small piece, for he knew that Barnabee, if he gave at all, would give sparingly; and he did not care to over do his character.

"You had better go, now; I hear some one coming. You may be discovered."

The girl hurried out of the room as fast as the darkness would allow. She had scarcely closed the door, when Barnabee entered at the opposite one, lamp in hand.

"I had forgotten there was no light in the room, Mr. Freel ve," said Barnabee, depositing the lamp and a roll of bank bills on the table. "But you are not afraid of the dark."

"My conscience has raised no ghost, as yet, sir. But the money—I am impatient."

The bills being large, they were soon counted, and the check given up therefore. Freelove then turned to Barnabee, his face livid with passion, and said,—

"I am out of thy power now, old man; take care you get not in mine. Be thou a thing accursed! May every dollar you have wrongfully taken from me turn to adders that shall sting you to your dying hour!"

Crushing his hat upon his head, Freelove left the room.

"Ha, ha, ha," laughed the old man, rubbing his hands in glee. "Two thousand dollars! A rare speculation! I must despatch John to collect the check as soon as the bank is open in the morning. Two thousand dollars! I can sleep soundly after this. Two thousand dollars!"

Thus exulting, Barnabee returned to his strong box to secure his treasure.

Arriving at his chamber, Freelove cast aside his disguise and struck a light.

"Now to see what Hebe favours the villain with her smiles."

The letter bore no address, neither was it sealed. Freelove opened it and read as follows:—

"I again require pecuniary assistance. Three hundred dollars will do. If you will bring it to me to-morrow evening, you will find me alone. Do not come till late, as I am to go out of town in the afternoon, in company with my brother and a friend of his, who possibly will stay till the evening. My maid will conduct you as usual."

It bore no name nor date; yet Freelove stood regarding it, his face pale as marble.

"It cannot be," at length he gasped. "And yet it must be! It bears no name, and yet it speaks as plain as words can speak. It is her hand-writing, beyond a shade of doubt."

He paced the room with rapid steps, and in a state of mind bodering on madness.

"It cannot be!" again he cried. "What could have induced her to listen, for a moment, to that horrid old man? She that is sought after by the first men in her circle. I must be worse than mad to doubt her thus! And yet," he continued, again examining the note, "I cannot doubt my eyes. Oh, this is maddening! My—, I cannot speak her name! and that detestable old man! If I had him now, I would not leave him till his dried up old carcase was food for dogs. What reason had she for such a step? She surely could not love him! No, that were harder to believe than her guilt. What then?—gold! No, no! she would not part with honour, virtue, that bright jewel of her sex, for gold! She cannot be so lost to shame, so dead to every principle of right, so—and why not? Have I not done as bad for gold? Oh, this is horrible, horrible!" and he sank into a chair, and covered his face with his hands.

Thus sitting, he thought the matter over more coolly. He asked himself what he should do. Should he seek her and at once accuse her? or should he wait and leave it to chance to throw more light upon it? If it could be kept still, and she avoid a public exposure, she might be reclaimed.

"But that old miserly villian," he exclaimed, "he shall pay dearly for this!"

CHAPTER V.

THE EXCURSION.

"And chiefly thou, O spirit, that dost prefer,
Before all temples, the upright heart and pure,
Instruct me ; for thou know'st."

THE afternoon following the events we have just related, at length arrived ; when, according to previous understanding, Helen, in company with Erwin, Freelove and Snooksby, were to visit Fresh Pond. The afternoon was fine, and the ride promised to be a pleasant one.

Freelove, although he had eight thousand dollars in pocket, was gloomy and thoughtful from the unpleasant affair that had come to his knowledge on the previous night ; but he was in part brought back to himself by the hilarity of Snooksby, who was quite himself—always happy when he could enjoy a "spree" at another's expense. But then, poor fellow, he was not to be blamed for being in "this breathing world ;" and being here without a silver spoon in his mouth, he must be fed at the public expense.

Erwin was also thoughtful, (as most people in love are,) having come to the determination to learn in the course of their afternoon's ride, what he had to expect from Helen. He had determined in the first place, to make her acquainted with the promise he gave his father ; to state to her his feelings—that he respected her ; but for love—that must form no part of their compact ; and then leave it for her to decide whether their union should take place, or not.

Helen, on the contrary, was all life and gaiety. How her fine face glowed with animated pleasure, when Erwin handed her into the phaeton and seated himself by her side ; how flashed her dark eyes at the fiery mettle of their spirited horse. Who, to look at her then—mark the brilliant flashes of her face, would have thought she concealed at her heart the canker-worm of remorse ;—that all that met the eye was put on ; and beneath was the dark midnight of an erring soul.

To horse, and away. The city was left behind, and the green fields and farm houses were flying with the speed of thought. Snooksby who had vainly tried to rouse Freelove to cheerfulness, at length attacked him in another quarter.

"I really believe, Tom, that you and Julia had a falling out last evening. You have been as sulky as a mad bull all day. How did she go to work to inflict that delicate wound on your face ? Not with her little hand, I'll be sworn. Come, give us to hear."

Freelove made no answer, but gave his ponies a touch of the "braid."

"You were out, I know," continued Snooksby, "for I called for you, thinking you might be polite enough to invite me out to supper, now that Phil has proved such a bore. Being not at home, you must have been somewhere else ; and if that somewhere else wasn't at dear Julia's, where the deuce was it ? You must have had a warm discussion, as the auguments seem to have been of a knock-down character."

"Snooksby, you are a fool !" exclaimed Freelove, exasperated beyond control.

"Unquestionably, my dear boy ; but like some foolish books, I have a d—d extravagant binding. By the way, speaking of binding, I begin to think that your ponies are nothing very binding, after all. You wanted my opinion, you know. Touch up the off one, Tom ; so—oh, they travel very well," he continued, eyeing the graceful animals, bounding away with the fleetness of the wind. "They travel very even, Tom, but rather lazy, you must confess. A little too much on the ox-team principle to be worth five hundred dollars."

"You are trying to make me angry, Snooksby, but you'll not succeed."

"The boy that fired an apple at the moon, did not succeed in hitting it, but he had the satisfaction of trying."

"You are a bore !"

"So others have told me before; but faith, you don't expect me to believe it. No, Tom; 'tis only that I am not understood. I love myself none the less because the vulgar world appreciates me not. Poor devils, that ye are! Were it not for me, the blue devils would reign supreme. But, like the sun, I make myself seen and felt ;—I shine out upon society, and scatter every cloud that darkens its horizon."

"For mercy's sake, Snooksby, stop that everlasting praise of self."

"My dear fellow, 'tis only that you are grouty. Do you know, Tom, I feel that I have much to be thankful for ?"

"In what, pray ?"

"In that Heaven takes not such as thee to itself, for then would Othello be deprived of his occupation."

While Freelove and Snooksby were thus wrangling like two overgrown schoolboys—Erwin and his companion were discoursing on a widely different subject. Their conversation at first was miscellaneous, and gradually took a turn towards the very subject Erwin had the most in thought.

"You were speaking," he said, "of a child's respect for the memory of its parent. I hold it as the most sacred duty we are called upon to obey. My mother died when I was too young to appreciate her worth, but my father lived to fill the place of both ; and to remember that dear friend is the dearest privilege I enjoy. His wishes I reverence next to the commands of God. And, indeed, it is to the fulfilment of a wish made to me on his dying bed, that I am called upon to learn your pleasure."

"Mine, Mr. Erwin !"

"Yes ; did you ever think seriously of getting married ?"

"Mr. Erwin !"

"Pardon me, Miss Freelove ! I am plain spoken, and little accustomed to frame words suited to a lady's ear. But if I am permitted, I will explain the affinity between the reverence I entertain for my father's wishes, yourself, and the question I have but now asked ; and trust you will take in kindness what at first appeared impertinent."

"I am listening, sir."

"Well, then ;—you need not be told that your father and mine were dear friends ; of that our younger days can bear testimony."

"Brothers could not be more loving."

"Entertaining such feelings for each other for more than forty years of their lives, it is not surprising that they should wish the union to be as close in their children."

"Say on,'" said Helen, almost breathless with expectation.

"Your father on his death-bed made the request to my father, that, when of sufficient age, we should be united."

"Did he make such a request ?"

"It was so told to me by my father, in his last moments. He then spoke of it as dear to his wishes likewise. I promised to obey him ; leaving it optional with you to accept or refuse my hand."

"You say obey. I infer from this that you entertain for me none of that warm feeling of love that our fathers wished to keep alive in their children."

"If I am accepted, I shall respect you as my wife, and shall endeavour to make our union a happy one."

"But you do not love me ?"

"That question is quite as direct as my first one."

"We are now dealing with facts."

"I must confess, then, I do not feel that love for you I once hoped to entertain for my wife, should I marry."

"Your candour does you credit, sir. The facts, then, are substantially these,

You make me a formal tender of your hand, solely because your father and mine desire the union to take place?"

Erwin was somewhat nettled that Helen should treat the matter thus coldly, and therefore replied as coldly,

"Solely, madam."

"And solely for the same reason, I accept it."

This was said in such a tone, that Erwin, astonished still more, could not re-

FREELOVE OBTAINING THE PROOF OF HIS SISTERS DISHONOUR.

frain from looking her full in the face, when Helen broke into a loud laugh. Pea after peal rang out, till the tears ran down her cheeks.

"Madam, this is unusual!" said Erwin, vexed still more. "It is not a subject for laughter."

"It is laughable because it is unusual! ha, ha, ha! I see you are offended, Mr Erwin; but I cannot help it. Who ever before put on such a long face at a sale"

"A sale, madam!"

"Yes, a sale, a *bona fide* sale; or, rather I should say, exchange of commo-

No. 7.

dities. Such as—here I am ; look at me ! A thing acted upon ; without a mind of my own ; without a heart ; but I will give myself in exchange for you, a thing in all respects as poor as I ; ha, ha, ha !"

"You are making me a jest."

"No, by my troth! I have been wanting to laugh all this morning. But come!" she continued, her manner suddenly changing, "I will be serious, and acknowledge that the honor you intend me in the offer of your hand, and the motive that prompted it, I fully appreciate and allow. And believe me when I say, I feel it a duty as sensibly as yourself, to acquiesce in the last wish of our parents ; and in the connection you have done me the favour to propose, I shall endeavour to make myself worthy your esteem."

The last few words were spoken with much feeling. Erwin was puzzled. One moment she was cold and respectful, the next spirited, sarcastic, and the moment after subdued with feelings apparently the most deep and heartfelt.

About this time they came in sight of St Mary's, and Erwin, (to dismiss a painful subject,) called Helen's attention to it, and spoke of it as one of the best institutions of the day. As they came near the grounds, Erwin observed a man entering the grove, whom he recognised as the Englishman he had seen twice before ; once on the stage-coach and again at the theatre.

Our little party soon reached Fresh Pond—it being but a few minutes' ride from St. Mary—but as nothing transpired worthy of record, we shall pass over it by saying that it went off pleasantly, and terminated with a sail, and collation on board the boat.

Erwin sought his bed early on that night, though not to sleep. His fate was now sealed beyond a possibility of change. Heretofore he had thought it more than probable Helen would refuse his hand ; but it was now past all hope ; and nothing was left him but the duty to make their union as happy as possible. He had been better satisfied, but he thought he saw Helen's motive in accepting him. It was not the desire to obey the wishes of her deceased parent, he thought ; but the advantage such a connection would give her to minister to her pleasures through his immense means.

CHAPTER XIII.

THE LUNCH.

A few days subsequent to the events recorded in the last chapter, as Erwin was passing up Tremont-street, he was accosted by Snooksby. Erwin felt in no mood to entertain that worthy hanger-on at every good man's table, (i. e. provided it was well stocked with eatables and drinkables,) for he had just returned from a morning's call on his future wife, and the more he tried to love her society, the more he was disenchanted with it, so perverse are all our feelings, so determined is the human heart (where love is concerned) to oppose the sounder judgment of the head, and set reason at defiance. Erwin would have passed on to his hotel, but Snooksby was not so easily avoided.

"Where are you bound, Phil?" he asked, coming up to him.

"I am returning to my room."

"There is nothing there ; not so much as a cup of coffee, or a boiled egg, neither a dried crust on which to starve a man, withal. I have just come from there. I sat myself down in the biggest chair in the room, rang the bell, and ordered breakfast ; and if you will believe it, the rascally servant would take no notice of me."

"I breakfasted four hours ago."

"You are a lucky fellow to get a breakfast at all in that house. Hereafter you may starve for them, for their larder is as empty as my stomach, and I hav'ent tasted food to-day. What do you say to calling on Bryden, and trying a dish of his New York oysters?"

"You must excuse me this morning, Mr. Snooksby," and Erwin took a step towards his hotel,

"Not I, by my hunger, which is intolerable. I have breakfasted, dined and supped with you for a fortnight; if you cannot do me the poor favour of a lunch, I'll eat no more with you. Besides, you will not be so well fed for the time to come."

"I fear I shall not," said Erwin, in a tone that meant more than Snooksby could understand.

"I'll swear you will not, for John Augustus Snooksby failed to draw from them—with all his assurance of future patronage, so much as would serve a rat withal. But come," he continued, slipping his arm through Erwin's, "you shall not deny me. The morn is fair, the time propitious, and the gods have made me deuced hungry."

Rather than be kept longer in the street, and as he could not shake Snooksby off without being intentionally rude, and thinking perhaps, he could get rid of him as cheaply by indulging him, Erwin followed him to Bryden', the famous man of the day, where oysters were concerned.

"How will you have them, gentlemen, cooked or raw?" asked an obsequious waiter, bowing and rubbing his hands.

"Raw, eh, Phil? Raw first, stewed after. Use dispatch, Jo, for I am as ravenous as a Roman Catholic after lent."

"Ay, ay, sir."

"Ha, ha; these are curious," said Snooksby, as soon as the oysters were placed before him. "Corn fed, eh, Jo? I take it these were manufactured expressly for Bryden. Use pepper and vinegar, Phil?"

"Both."

"So do I. I think they are damnably insipid alone. Nature's mouth was deucedly out of taste when she flavoured the oyster."

"Perhaps she didn't knew anything about pepper and vinegar when she invented them," suggested Jo.

"You can go about your business, Jo. When we want anything more we will call."

"Ay, ay, sir."

Snooksby swallowed half a dozen oysters, smacked his lips, and then asked,—

"Do you go to L—'s to-night?"

"I haven't been invited."

"Neither have I. Ha—r—r—r! this vinegar is as strong as the devil. It was an oversight in them in not inviting me. Where do you go?"

"I shall not go out to-night."

"Not go out, Phil! The gods write thee down an ass, then. I will spend the evening with you, as I have no engagement."

"I cannot avail myself of your kind offer," said Erwin coldly. "I am engaged to-night."

"You are not well, I think; now I look at you, you seem dispirited. Give me to know the cause of your distress."

"You are very kind, sir, but you will pardon me if I keep my own counsel."

"Oh, certainly, if you desire it. Waiter, more oysters. Phil, you will have another dish?"

"With your leave I withdraw."

"You are not going yet?"

"By your leave."

Erwin rose to his feet.

"Why, if you insist," said Snooksby; "but really, Phil, I must have another plate. You know I haven't breakfasted."

"Don't let my departure disturb you,"

"I declare, Phil—really—I do believe I have left my purse at home," said Snooksby, feeling in all his pockets.

Erwin threw a piece of money on the table, and left the room.

"I'm devilish glad he took the hint," said Snooksby, "for I haven't a fip to lay my jaws to," and then he stooped to pick up a letter which he saw drop from Erwin's hat as he left the shop. It was addressed to "Philip Erwin, Esq., Boston, Tremont House."

Snooksby unhesitatingly opened it. When he had read it, he gave a long, low whistle, by way of expressing his astonishment, and put the letter in his pocket.

"Here's a discovery," he said, at the same time letting an oyster slip down the avenue to his stomach. "I don't wonder Phil is down-hearted, poor fellow! Well, it is truly said, 'Fortune is a fickle goddess;' though truth to say, I have no just cause to complain of her constancy. She has been constantly frowning on me."

Snooksby soon after finished his oysters, left the room, and took the nearest way to Mount Vernon-street. He met Freelove on the steps, going out.

"One moment, Tom," he cried, as soon as he came up. "I have discovered something that nearly concerns us all. Is Helen in?"

"I have just left her; but mark me, Snooksby, I am in no mood for foolery; my temper is somewhat sour of late."

"I have tasted it sufficiently, of late."

"If you have anything I shall care to hear, I will go back."

"You shall hear full soon."

This was said while Snooksby was ascending the front stairs to the parlour. Freelove followed. Snooksby entered the parlour without noticing Helen, who was somewhat surprised by his hurried entrance, and cast himself upon the sofa.

"I have walked so fast I am all out of breath," were his first words, wiping the perspiration from his forehead. "Poor fellow, he's in a bad way."

Helen could hardly refrain from laughing at Snooksby's earnest manner.

"Have you gone mad, Mr. Snooksby?"

"Would to the gods I had, ere I learned this of my friend."

"What has happened to your friend?" asked Freelove, impatient at being detained.

"Everything! The very worst of ills that could befal mortal man. Houses, barns, lands, goods, and chattels; everything; all gone."

"Who is so unfortunate?"

"Who? Phil Erwin, to be sure."

Freelove and Helen turned instantly pale, and exchanged quick glances.

"You shall hear," said Snooksby, taking the letter Erwin had dropped in the oyster room from his pocket.

"——ville, June 16, 18—.

"DEAR SIR:—I regret to inform you, that on examination of your deceased father's papers, and looking over the town books, I have discovered (what did not at first appear) that his property was very much embarrassed. It were best, perhaps, that I should write plainly. You are a beggar. The large estate on which your father resided is mortgaged for more than its present value; the large amount of stocks in his possession were held by him only in trust; in short, there is not enough remaining, of all I can scrape together. to satisfy your last draft on me. You had better return home to ——ville, as soon as possible.

"I am, with respect, your friend and obedient servant,

"Philip Erwin, Esq."   "NATHANIEL LAW."

"How did that come into your possession?" asked Freelove, catching the letter from Snooksby, and hurriedly running it over again.

"You shall have it in six words. Half an hour ago, I met Phil in the street; he seemed dejected, and to raise his spirits, I invited him into Bryden's for a plate of oysters. I chatted and talked, as usual; I laughed and I swore, but all to no effect; his face would be long in spite of me. At length I hinted that there might be some cause for it. At this hint he spoke, and being ashamed to betray such feelings in my presence, he caught up his hat and rushed out of the room."

" But this letter ?"

"It dropped from his hat as he went out. I called after him, but could not make him hear; so, thinking it no harm, as I am his bosom friend, I just looked into it."

" This is indeed unfortunate for our friend Erwin," said Freelove, as a poor attempt to disguise his agitated feelings. " But we must not let his misfortunes put a damper on our feelings, or take away our appetite. You will dine with me to-day, Snooksby ?"

" Why, thank you, I'm not particularly engaged elsewhere."

" I am for the present; so if you will do me the favour to step down to the colonel's and order dinner at my expense, I will join you at two."

This was done on the part of Freelove evidently to get rid of Snooksby, who needed no second invitation nor urging to bespeak the dinner, but at once forgetting his friend's misfortune in his own good fortune—getting an invitation to dine out—left the house.

As soon as Snooksby had left the room, Freelove sunk upon the sofa, and sat the picture of disappointment.

"So much for our scheming!" at length he said, bitterly. "So much for all our crouching and fawning ! I do believe the devil is in league against us !"

" Brother, I need not marry this man now?" said Helen.

" Know you of no reason why you should marry him, or some one else ?" asked Freelove, sharply, turning quickly upon his sister.

" None."

" None ! are you quite sure ? Think again."

" Quite !" she answered, slightly colouring. " What mean you, brother ?"

" Mean, girl !" he cried, starting to his feet, as if fixed upon some determined purpose ;—he faltered, and only said,—

" Nothing, nothing ! you can do as you think proper about marrying him !"

Freelove left the house.

* * * * * *

A few minutes after two o'clock, a note was handed Erwin, in his room, by a servant. He broke the seal; and read as follows :—

Mount Vernon Street, Two o'clock.

DEAR SIR.—A few days since, I gave you encouragement that your suit for my hand might, after mature deliberation, be accepted. I have to inform you that, on thinking the subject over calmly, I believe such an union would be attended with unhappy results to both of us ; and as I hold my happiness paramount to any and every consideration you can urge in favour of the connection, I beg leave, unconditionally, to decline the honour you intend me. With a desire that I may retain your friendship, I remain, your friend,

" HELEN FREELOVE."

" Fate, I thank thee for this !" exclaimed Erwin, refolding the letter. "Oh, my father !" he continued, fervently, " if from thy high throne thou art permitted to look down upon thy son in this world, surely thou wilt forgive him this deception, when thou seest the load it has raised from off his heart—the new spring of hope gushing forth, that shall make life a blessing."

CHAPTER XIV.

THE DISCOVERY.

HELEN was alone in her room. She sat by the window, her face buried in the folds of the rich drapery curtains, her bowed form agitated by the most powerful emotion.

"I have been a fool!" she said, at length, raising her face from the damask, wet with scalding tears, wrung from a tortured heart, conscious that it has been its own worst enemy. "I have trifled with one who must despise me for the part I have played, oh! how meanly, for the sake of that gold which as often brings with it a curse as a blessing. And worse, oh, God; for gold I have been the base pander to an old man's pleasure—a miser! who gives me grudgingly what I have earned so dearly. I sent my maid to him with a note nearly a week since, asking for the paltry sum of three hundred dollars, and I have not heard from him yet. My brother, too, has nothing for me of late, but harsh words and sour looks. I am deserted by every one. And if, as I fear, I am—I cannot speak the word! oh, what will become of me? I shall die with shame!" And again she buried her face in the friendly concealment of the window-curtain.

After a long hour of weeping, Helen rose more calm. Providing herself with materials, she wrote a short note in pencil, and then rang for her maid.

"Mary," she said, as the maid entered the room, averting her face so that she should not see she had been weeping. "Are you sure Mr. Barnabee got my last note?"

"I put it into his own hands, marm."

"I fear you made some mistake. See that you give him this."

"Yes, marm."

"Stay! Let no one see you enter; be discreet, and you shall be better rewarded in the future."

"Thank ye, marm. He gave me a shilling piece the last time I went."

"You shall be remembered for the future, if you continue to serve me faithfully. Be sure, above all things, that you put this note into his own hands."

"You may be sure I will."

With the last word the maid left the room. She quickly attired herself, and descended the stairs into the entry. She there met Freelove, who entered at the moment from his dinner at the colonel's, not a little flushed with wine.

"Where do you go, mistress?" he asked sharply, on seeing Mary bonneted to go out.

"I am going out for a moment, if you please, sir, for Miss Helen."

"Step into the parlour, I wish to have minute's talk with you."

"If you please, sir, Miss Helen is in haste." said the girl, trembling.

"Do you hear me? I wish to have a talk with you," he said, still more sharply, pointing to the parlour door.

Mary did not dare to do otherwise than obey. Freelove secured the door, and approaching the girl, who was trembling like an aspen leaf, he said,—

"Where were you last Thursday night?"

"I, sir! I was at home."

"Did you not go out?"

"I go out, sir?"

"Yes, you. You were seen to leave the house after ten o'clock. What sent you out late?"

I—I—go out—late, sir?"

"Come, come ! have done with your stammering, and answer my questions intelligibly. What sent you out so late, and where did you go ?"

" I'll die before I'll tell," said the girl, seeing she was cornered and could not evade the question.

"Have a care, mistress," said Freelove, severely. "We have laws that will punish your temerity. You forget you cannot always do as you choose without being called to an account for it. Tell me where you went last Thursday night."

" I will not ! that's flat."

Freelove ground his teeth with rage.

" I'll find a way to tame you, miss. I know more than you think. You have acknowledged you went out ; now tell me where you went."

The girl was silent.

" You were the bearer of a note," continued Freelove.

" A note !" gasped the girl.

"Ay, a note. See if that will refresh your memory." And Freelove handed her the note that was placed in his hands by the unknown person, while he was waiting for his money at Barnabee's."

The girl took the note, tremblingly opened it, and burst into tears.

" You see I know more than you at first supposed."

" He ought to be ashamed of himself to let you have that letter," sobbed the girl.

"The old rascal is not guilty of any such honesty. He has not seen the letter."

" He has, for I put it into his own hand."

" Oh-o-o-o! you acknowledge it, then ?"

The girl seeing she had betrayed herself, redoubled her tears.

" I could not help it—you made me tell."

" Murder will out, traitress ; Now what do you expect for the part you have played in this affair ? Do you not deserve punishment for aiding in the ruin of my sister ?"

" I had nothing to do with it, indeed I had not."

"'Tis false, girl ! you let the old rascal in and out."

" Miss Helen told me to do so."

" How long has he vis—visited her ?"

" Four or five months, sir."

" How many times have you been to his den for money ?"

"Only a few—times, sir."

" You were going there, now ?"

Th girl was silent.

" Do you hear? where is the note you were to give him ?"

" Indeed, indeed, sir ! I cannot let you have it."

" Give me the note !"

"Mercy, mercy ! do not look so terrible !"

" Will you give me the note, girl ?" exclaimed Freelove, grasping her tightly by the arm.

" I might as well die one way as another," she said, giving him the note ; and bursting again into tears, she left the room.

Freelove hastily tore open the note, and read as follows :—

" A few days since, I sent my maid to you with a note, asking for a small sum of money, and have not heard from you since. The cause of this delay I cannot understand, though no doubt you have good reason for your silence. Please to send me the sum required, which is the least you can do. Gold is a poor recompense for what I daily suffer for my imprudence. I fear the worst of evils! I fear I am soon to be a mother. Should my fears prove true, Heaven only knows what will become of me."

Freelove's anger knew no bounds on reading this note, penned but a few minutes before by his unhappy sister. The wine he had drunk helped not a little to inflame his blood, and magnify the wrong towards himself. He thought less of the wrongs his sister had suffered than of the wound in his pride. He thought not of pouring the oil of pity into her bleeding bosom, which, nevertheless, needed such consolation, however foolishly she had brought the misery upon herself.

Pale with rage, mad with the combined effort of wine and wounded vanity, he took the way to his sister's chamber.

When Mary left Freelove, she rushed up stairs, and threw herself at Helen's feet.

"I could not help it, indeed, I could not help it!" she cried. "Kill me if you will, but I could not help it!"

"What has happened, Mary?"

"It was no fault of mine, indeed, it was not. He took it from me!"

"What mean you? the—the note?"

"He pinched my arm till it was black and blue."

"Who did this?"

"Your brother, marm; I hear him coming now. He's found it all out somehow, but I did not tell him."

It was at this moment that Freelove, exasperated in the manner we have described, entered his sister's room. Helen, guessing the worst, drew herself up to her full height, and stood waiting him, her face and lips as colourless as marble.

Freelove stood a moment at the door, with eyes fixed upon her, withering in their glance; but her pale face gave no token of his presence, save her eyes were bent upon the floor, and her bosom heaved like the silent swelling of the sea.

In the brief space of a few seconds, who shall say what passed through the mind of that brother and sister? who picture the resentment of the one, having no sympathy for an erring sister—himself the more faulty,—who tell of the burning shame of the other, her deep throes and remorseful conscience?

"So, miss," thundered out Freelove, "I have found you out at last; your base actions at length are known. The damning stain you have brought upon our family, is——"

"Hold, sir!" exclaimed Helen, calmly, and yet commandingly. "It is not for you to accuse me. Let it not be said a brother published a sister's shame." And then motioning Mary to leave the room, she continued, "You have found me out at last, you say; you have discovered that I am unworthy to be called the daughter of your father; I grant it."

"I am glad you are sensible of the disgrace you have brought upon me."

"No one can have a worse opinion of me, not even thyself, brother, than I entertain for myself. No one can look upon Helen Freelove with more contempt than I do. I do not hope to escape your anger, I am worthy of all you can say of me; but let not others hear thy reproaches, brother. For the sake of the dear memory of our father and our mother, let not my name meet with shame."

Freelove was silenced. He marked the quivering lip, and the crystal drops trembling on his sister's eyelids, and in spite of his efforts to the contrary, he was softened towards her.

"You should have thought of this before," he said.

"I should indeed, brother; and yet how few in the giddy mass of society—borne along in the swift current of excitement, pause to reflect—when temptations are thrown in their path, look to the end. Oh! I have suffered beyond the power of utterance. The very moment the rash step was taken, I felt I was lost, and every succeeding day has brought fresh evidence of its truth, to weigh me down to earth. I have laughed when my heart was breaking with its load of shame; I have carried a smiling face when darkness brooded over every corner of my soul; and all this from one false step, taken for gold; and I am lost, lost!" And she sank upon the sofa, and again gave herself up for lost.

"How came all this about, Helen?"

"He came here first to see you on business. You wanted money, and he supplied you with it. It was then I had the misfortune to attract his notice. I, too, needed money to keep up my position in society. He was rich, and—and—you know the rest."

"The old robber! the black-hearted, dastardly old villain!" muttered Freelove, between his teeth. "He has robbed me of my wealth, and my sister of her happiness. If I am spared, I will call him to a dread account for this."

"Do nothing to endanger our reputation, I implore you, brother! I am the guilty one, let me suffer for it."

LADY MANLY FAINTING AT THE TALE OF SIR RICHARD SAVILE,

"If you have done wrong, it does not make him the less guilty. He took advantage of your necessities, as he has of mine; and if there be a God in heaven, I will have vengeance. I have an account of my own to settle as well as yours."

Freelove left the room.

When alone, the unhappy girl, no longer able to hold back, gave herself up to unrestrained tears of unavailing sorrow.

No. 8.

CHAPTER XV.

THE RELIC.

> " All the world's a stage,
> And all the men and women merely players :
> They have their exits and their entrances ;
> And one man in his time plays many parts.''

ON the morning of the day these scenes were enacting, events of no slight moment to our story were taking place at St Mary.

"Annie, my child," said Madame Jerome, on the morning referred to, " you are this day eighteen. This is the sixteenth birthday you have passed under my care; and I wish, on this occasion, to have some conversation with you. Sit down, my child, here—at my feet.

" I have observed of late, my child," continued Madame Jerome, " that you are unhappy. With pain I have witnessed your cheek paling day by day—have seen the tears start unbidden to your eye, at some fancied kindness from me—have marked the change in your habits. You go not out now, as you used to go, and spend hours in the grove ; but confine yourself to the duties of the asylum, or shut yourself up for a whole day in your chamber. Why is this, my child ?"

" Mother.''

" I should have spoken of this before, only that I was waiting for this day, that we might both make a clean breast. That if I had in any way offended——''

" Oh, no, no, no !''

" I might be forgiven, and if you had any hidden sorrow, you might share it with one who would sympathise with thee as a mother with a dear child. What is the cause of your unhappiness, my child ?''

" Do not ask me, mother, for I cannot tell you.''

" Not tell me, Annie ?''

" I would tell you, dear mother, if I could tell any one. It is a foolish whim I shall soon forget. I am not very unhappy, dear mother ; 'tis only that your tender care magnifies all you see.''

" Might I not guess at the cause, my child ? I trust love has nothing to do with it.''

Annie looked quickly up in Madame Jerome's face, to see how she should understand her ; and seeing something that told her that her secret was betrayed, she blushingly turned away, and her eyes sought the floor.

" I have thought so for some days," said the kind-hearted woman. "But love should not make you unhappy, my child, unless, indeed, you love one unworthy of thee, or love hopelessly. Who is it you regard so dearly ? 'Tis nothing you should be ashamed of, unless, as I said, you love unworthily ; and I do not fear, my child, in that respect. Who is it, Annie? Is it Charles ?" she asked, after a pause of some moments.

" Oh no !'' said the girl, looking her ingenuously in the face. " I love him only as a brother ; but I believe he has forgotten me ; he has not been here for several days.''

The reader is aware that Annie knew nothing of Charles's intended tour abroad ; for it was at the time she received such rough treatment at the hands of Slickham and his disguised accomplice—Freelove—that he had desired her to meet him, to bid her farewell.

" I can think of but one other whom you would be likely to love, my child,'' continued Madame Jerome. " It may be Mr. Erwin.''

The blush mantling still deeper on Annie's cheek convinced Madame Jerome she was right in her suspicions.

"Cherish him in thy love, my child, he is worthy of thee."

"How strangely you talk, mother; is it not wrong to love before you are asked to love? He never will love me."

"Does not our Heavenly Father love us without our asking for his love? Does not a mother love her offspring without being asked? Love is always the same, though differing in its object. How know you he loves you not; did he ever tell you so?"

'Oh, mother! you know he never did; he has never addressed a word to me except in your presence.'

"Mr. Erwin will be here to-day," said Madame Jerome, in a tone that made the blood leap in the young girl's veins.

"I must remind you again," continued Madame Jerome, "that this is your birth day; and the day on which, in accordance with the duties imposed upon me I am to put into your hands a paper that will throw some light upon your parentage."

"A paper for me! you never mentioned it before."

"No, my child; by your mother's request, I was to place it in your hand on your eighteenth birthday."

"You have seen my mother then?"

"She was a dear and intimate friend of mine. I was with her when she bid farewell to this world and its sorrows, for ever, and made her a solemn promise, to watch faithfully over the happiness of her child, and cherish it as my own."

"How nobly you have kept your promise, my more than mother. But my father, did you know him, too?"

"I am not permitted to speak of him, my child; but undoubtedly the package will give you all the information you desire."

Madame Jerome then went to a small box and took from it the package. It was of the size of a large letter, but much thicker, having the appearance of several sheets of paper folded together—wound about with a narrow black ribbon—carefully sealed.

"Take this, my child," said Madame Jerome, placing the package in Annie's hand, "and whatever it may disclose of the follies and sufferings of your parents, exercise towards them that feeling of forgiveness and commiseration their fates require."

The tears started into Madame Jerome's eyes as she said this, and she hastily left the room.

It was with a trembling hand Annie took this relic of her mother. It seemed to her a voice from the past—the unforgotten dead, giving her that knowledge of her parents she had so long lived in ignorance of.

She could not open it in Madame Jerome's room; the duty was too sacred to be intruded upon. She would hasten to her favourite seat in the grove, where no eye, save God's, could look upon that communion of mother and daughter.

A minute, and she was seated on the rude bench that had kindly borne her weight from childhood, and protected from the sun by the friendly shelter of the trees; she broke the seal affixed by a dying mother's hand sixteen years before. She opened the package and the miniature of a gentleman, set in brilliants, fell into her lap.

"Can this be the likeness of my father!" she thought, gazing at the cold picture. "How noble he looks—how proud, and there is a benevolent beaming in the eye that tells of a good heart. He has an open brow and a fine expressive mouth," she said, admiringly. "And this is my father, whom mysterious fate deprived me of before I could gladden his heart with the lisping of his name. But why, dear mother, did you not leave your likeness too; that I might gaze upon it side by side with my father; and worship the cold ivory, being deprived of thyself and him."

And then kissing her father's picture, she laid it carefully upon the seat beside her and opened her mother's manuscript.

CHAPTER XVI.

A LOOK AT THE PAST.

"Angels and ministers of grace defend us !
Be thou a spirit of health or goblin damn'd,
Bring'st with thee airs from heaven or blasts from hell,
Be thy intent wicked, or charitable,
Thou com'st in such a questionable shape,
That I will speak to thee.   I'll call thee, Hamlet,
King, Father, Royal Dane; Oh, answer me ;
Let me not burst in ignorance ; but tell,
Why thy canoniz'd bones, hearsed in death,
Have burst their cerements?   Why the sepulchre,
Wherein we saw thee quietly inurned,
Hath op'd his ponderous and marble jaws,
To cast thee up again?"

FEELING that this—one day—will meet my daughter's eye, in justice to the memory I would have her cherish of her unhappy mother, I will set before her that portion of my history, which involved the greatest share of happiness I enjoyed in this world and all the misery fate stored up for me.   And that my child may judge of me fairly and impartially, I will go back to the time when I was yet a maiden and follow on, leaving out nothing that might speak against me, nor add anything that might do wrong to others.

I was the daughter of a gentleman, residing in ———shire, but a few miles from London.   My father was possessed of a considerable estate, which enabled us to live in a style suiting my most extravagant fancy, and receive much company.

Among the hundreds that visited my father's mansion, was Lord Manly.   He was a gentleman of sober habits and moral worth—was possessed of a large revenue, and, moreover, was a very handsome man ; but, with all, was no favourite with my father.

There was another, Sir Richard Savile, (I mention these two gentlemen because, as you will see in the sequel of my story, the skein of my destiny was fatedly woven with theirs,) who was particularly favoured by my father.   He was rich and respected among men, but he bore about him that ineffable something that rendered him unpleasing in my sight.

Both of these gentlemen were suitors for my hand.   My father left me free to choose between them, but gave me freely to understand that he would be better pleased should I prefer Sir Richard Savile.

But it was impossible, with the noble, manly and accomplished Lord Manly and the conceited Richard Savile before me, I should hesitate to choose, and in less than three months I was the wife of Ernest Manly.

Then followed the gaieties of the London season, and at the opera, play, or route, I had but one companion and he my husband.   I heard of Richard Savile, indeed, as being quite a lion at Almack's, and at Lady C———'s and Lady L———'s parties, but we never met. Spring came, and with it the news of my father's death, after the short illness of two days.

He was my only surviving parent, and when he died, I followed to the tomb the best friend, save my husband, I then had.   We did not return to the metropolis again, for I had no heart for the city life, but longed rather for retirement, and followed my husband to his estate in ———shire, where I shortly after gave birth to a daughter. We did not go to London the next winter, for I found more enjoyment in doing for my little Annie, and listening to her sweet prattle, than in all the artificial excitement society gives.

My husband, too, was with me. He was gay, attentive, and apparently happy; and the hours shared with him and our child were without alloy. Oh, I look back to those calm days of sunshine, as to the few fleeting moments of a blissful dream, for like the sun-fly basking upon the bosom of a crystal fountain—its life is of a span's length.

At length, one day, when you were a little more than a year old, my husband announced his determination to go to town. I was a little surprised that he did not explain the nature of the business that called him away from me, but as he did not see fit to acquaint me with it, I did not question him.

It was the first time he had left me since our marriage, and be sure I counted each hour till his promised return. It came at last—but Ernest came not with it, neither did he send a line to account for his longer absence. That night, how closely I pressed my little Annie to my heart, and breathing a prayer for her father's safety, I passed the long hours of sleepless night, but I did not then once dream he could be false to me. No; I would have blistered my tongue had it given utterance to such a thought.

The next morning my maid presented me with a card, saying that the gentleman was below. It was Sir Richard Savile. I could not receive him, I thought. I was ill; besides, I had been weeping, and my eyes were red. I was not prepared to receive him. And yet I thought I must. I had not seen him since my marriage, and he was my father's most intimate friend. I must treat him with respect at least; I would receive him out of love for my father. I requested my maid to desire him to walk up.

He was very sociable, talked much of my husband, said he had never visited his estate before; but there was something in his manner that displeased me—a certain free way of examining my face, that made me blush to my temples. I thought he saw I was unhappy.

"Lord Manly is in London," he said.

I assented, though truth to say, I did not know where he was.

"The London season is quite over, though the L——'s have not left town. The young ladies were favourites of Lord Manly."

"I have heard him speak of them," I replied, "but I never had the pleasure of their acquaintance."

"They would have been dangerous rivals to your ladyship, especially Lady Ann. She is a perfect Hebe in her way."

I took no notice of this ungallant speech, and after half an hour's light conversation, poorly sustained on my part, Sir Richard rose to take his leave. I could do no less than invite him to remain for dinner, but he politely refused, saying that he should be some days in the neighbourhood, and should be happy to avail himself of the invitation when Lord Manly returned.

There was nothing in this conversation that should make me unhappy, yet owing to the low state of my feelings, every word went to my heart. I passed the whole day between hope and fear. Fear suggested that something serious had happened to him, or he never would have stayed away so long without sending me some word to reassure me; and hope whispered, cheer up, he will be the bearer of his own kind words, and so passed the day.

About five o'clock the London morning papers arrived. I eagerly examined every line, thinking I should meet with his name. My labours were rewarded, but it only added fuel to my unhappiness. The paragraph did not explain the business that detained him; but only a few lines, giving an account of a splendid ball, the last of the season, given by the Duchess G——, and Lord Manly's name was mentioned with that of Lady Ann L——, in terms not very flattering to the honour or happiness of his wife.

"I can see it all," I thought. "He has tired of me and the secluded life he leads in the country. I am no longer sufficient for his happiness. He has tired of you, my child," I said, catching up my little Annie, who was playing on the floor, and I wept over her as passionately as if her cruel father had indeed deserted us.

In the evening Sir Richard Savile was announced, and entered the room before I could give orders that I was indisposed, and could not be seen. The room I occupied was on the first floor, and the windows were low, and looked out upon the park. I am particular in mentioning this fact, for reasons you will see anon.

I was weeping, with my little Annie in my lap, when Sir Richard entered the room. He seemed surprised, and apologised for his intrusion. I desired him to be seated.

"Your ladyship is lonely, I fear," he said, "without the society of Lord Manly. Has his lordship been long in town?"

"But a short time," I answered, not raising my eyes from the floor, for I felt my feelings would betray me.

"I marvel that Lord Manly took not your ladyship along with him. Your ladyship would have been a fair addition to the circle now in town."

"Your words mean something, Sir Richard," I exclaimed, starting up, for I was in that state of nervous excitement that grasped at possibilities. "Tell me if you know aught of my husband. Speak!"

"Calm yourself, dear Lady Manly," he said, soothingly. "The affair is not so bad as you imagine, perhaps. Lord Manly has indeed been imprudent, but I trust, for your happiness, he can satisfactorily explain himself."

"You are preparing me for some dreadful news, Sir Richard. For mercy sake keep me not in suspense! Tell me the worst at once!"

"I received a letter by this evening's post from Lord W——. You are acquainted with Lord W——?"

"Yes, yes," I gasped.

"It is a confidential letter, and meant only for my reading; but in consideration to your feelings, you shall see it."

Sir Richard then took from his pocket the letter, of which I give you an extract as nearly as I can remember.

"Speaking of news, my dear Savile, there is as pretty a piece of scandal afloat here as I have heard of this many a day; containing matter enough, egad, to keep all the old grandams in Christendom chewing for a twelvemonth. You know Lord Manly, a bold, handsome fellow, the very pink of propriety, and yet there is a little of the sly Quaker about him. It was at the Duchess G——'s ball, where Manly had contrived to make himself agreeable in the eyes of Lady Ann, the youngest daughter of Lady L——, a small bunch of coquetry, by the way, to the no little annoyance of Lord T——, whom the little enchantress had favoured with her smiles on some previous occasion.

"At length, Lord T——, no longer able to conceal the green-eyed monster that had taken possession of his brain, after making several fruitless attempts to draw Lady Ann away from his more favoured rival, stepped up to Manly, and said, loud enough to be heard by several ladies and gentleman present, "Of what colour, my lord, are the curtains of Madame Guizot's bed-chamber?" (Madame Guizot, as you know, is a French opera singer.) Whereupon Lord Manly struck Lord T—— in the face; and the confusion that followed was a caution to all lovers of harmony. Upon this it crept out that Lord Manly pressed the couch nightly, with the fair Guizot."

I could read no more. The excitement that my strength had fed upon thus far suddenly gave way, and I swooned.

When I recovered, I found Sir Richard bending over me, his face expressing the deepest commiseration for my wrongs. He soon after took his leave, and I, heart-broken, sought again a sleepless pillow.

The next morning I received a note from my husband, full of bitterness and wrath, calling me the most cruel names, and commanding me instantly to leave the country, with my child. It said he should not return until I had left his house for ever, and said he would make provision for our support in any country I might adopt as my home, and limited my stay in his house to three days.

This last piece of cruelty I did not expect from my husband. What had I done, that I should be driven from my home and country—an exile in some foreign land? It was true, I had but little now to bind me to England. My parents were both dead, and all others of my surviving relatives were distant and little known to me.

" I will obey him," I said, pressing my child, now dearer to me than ever, to my almost broken heart. "We will leave his house, my child, and seek that protection in the land of ' Freedom ' denied to us here. May the God of the widow and the fatherless be our stay."

In the afternoon Sir Richard called again. I told him of the cruel letter I had received from my husband. He seemed greatly surprised, and asked me what I intended to do. I answered that I had ever endeavoured to obey the slightest wish of my husband, and that I should not disobey him in this.

On telling of the country I had chosen for my home, (America,)he volunteered to procure me a passage in the first sailing vessel, and provide for my comfort and support. Soon after this, Sir Richard left me.

In the evening I received a note from him, informing me that a vessel was to sail for Charleston, S. C., in the morning, and that he had taken passage in it for me and my child; and desired me to make instant preparation for my journey, as I might be called for at a moment's warning.

With a sinking heart I went about the desired preparations; for I was leaving the spot where I had passed the happiest hours of my life, and was bound on a journey, at any time not very desirable, and now to be full of gloom and misdoubting. My preparations were soon finished, for my child's and my wardrobe was easily packed; these, with my jewels and what ready money I had at my command, were all I proposed to take with me, for I scorned to receive that support his insulting letter spoke of, when he had cast me off so cruelly.

Sir Richard was at the door very early the following morning, with a carriage. He was pale and appeared much excited; but I was too much agitated myself to remark upon it. In five minutes I had bidden farewell to my home for ever, and in five minutes more on board the vessel. Assisting me into the cabin, Sir Richard hastily pressed my hand, bade me farewell, and disappeared.

CHAPTER XVII.

THE MSS. CONTINUED.

" Now in the fervid noon the smooth bright sea
  Heaves slowly for the wandering winds are dead
  That stirred it into foam. The lonely ship
  Rolls wearily, and idly flap the sails
  Against the creaking masts. The lightest sound
  Is lost not on the ear, and things minute
  Attract the observant eye."

IT was some weeks before I could go on deck, from sea-sickness. One evening, leaving Annie asleep, with my maid, who had consented to accompany me, I ventured up, for it had been hot and sultry throughout the day, with little or no wind.

Oh, it was a beautiful sight! I remember it well. The round full moon was high in the heavens; the stars gazed down like eyes of love, watching our frail bark sitting like a bird upon the silent waters. The wind was dead, and all hushed to profound stillness. I could almost hear my heart beat. Above, beneath, around, I was present with God. I leaned upon the railing, and for a half-hour gazed upon the moon-lit waters with feelings calmed in unison with the lovely scene.

I was only reminded of the length of my stay, when footsteps approached the quarter deck, and a man stood by my side. Imagine my surprise; it was Sir Richard Savile.

"I did not tell you I was to be your fellow-voyager," he said, "for fear you would deny me. But I could not consent that you should go to a strange country without one friend in your exile."

"You are very good," I replied, "but it was unnecessary. I shall not lack friends; God has promised to befriend those who call upon him."

"Such confidence is worthy your pure heart, my dear Lady Manly. Still it argues little for your knowledge of the world."

"I know I have trials before me, and they will be many; but it has been said, and I believe its truth, that a 'mother, bearing her infant in her arms, has Nature's passport through the world.' I do not despair of finding those who will respect my rights, and I shall find me an asylum in the new world, where I may pass my days in quiet, and rear my child as one of Freedom's daughters."

Soon after this conversation, I went below. I saw Sir Richard but a few times during the remainder of the voyage. He was respectful and kind, and sent several times to inquire after my health.

On arriving at Charleston, I took rooms at an hotel, and began to consider what I should do. If I should dispose of my jewels, I should have sufficient means to live upon, and insure my child a competency when I was gone. This I desired to do, and began to look about me for a small house, suiting my taste, and one that would allow me to live within the sum I had allowed for my yearly support.

Sir Richard, when he had learned my plan, aided me in my search, and we were not long in finding one, all I could wish, but a few miles from the city. It was a lovely spot; surrounded by every variety of fruit trees, and here I hoped to live, forgetting and forgotten.

Sir Richard often came out to see me—was very friendly, and seemed to take great interest in my little Annie. But why need I dwell upon his attentions; which too soon, alas! became downright boldness. I too soon discovered his true character, and the object he had in following me to America.

At length, one day when fired beyond endurance at his insulting proposals, I forbade him my presence, and desired him never again to enter my house. He received my words with provoking coolness, and informed me that it was my house no longer; that he was master—and so it proved. He had bought over my maid, and I was a prisoner in my own house.

Day after day we kept up the war of words, until at length his patience became entirely exhausted, and the devil of his nature predominated, and he then unfolded the whole diabolical scheme by which he had accomplished my ruin. Exultingly he cried,—

"Lord Manly was not false to thee."

"Not false?"

"I have said it."

"Where then was he when—"

"At London. I did not deceive thee in that."

"What business could he have, that he should keep a secret from his wife?"

"It involved the honour of a dear friend. He was detained longer than he expected, and wrote you several letters. I intercepted them. The paragraph in the paper was inserted by me, and the letter I read you from Lord W—— was all a forgery."

"O God!"

"With a view to your separation, I contrived, by my accomplices, to inflame

Lord Manly with a doubt of your virtue ; in a word, that you privately received visits from me."

" Monster."

" Manly affected to treat it all as a farce, but one could see he was burning at his heart. He had not received a line from you in answer to his letters, and as jealous as I had contrived to render thee, he hastened home."

" Did he come home ?"

FREELOVE PUTS BARNABEE TO THE TORTURE.

" On entering the park, and reining up before his house, through the window he saw thee in my arms. Ha, ha, ha ! this was all he needed to set his brain on fire. O, Lord Manly! Though he was a man of violent feelings, he was possessed of sterling principles," continued Savile scornfully. " He could not brook the slightest stain upon his unsullied honour. He turned and left the park, and left thee, ha, ha, as he supposed, in the arms of your seducer."

" Oh if he had but entered and confronted me ; if he had asked an explanation ; if he had spoken but one word, all would have been well. He would now be happy, and I spared the misery of this hour."

No. 9.

"The next morning he sent you that kind worded letter that put you entirely in my power; and with the same pen he wrote me a challenge."

"And you met—"

"On the very morning that I so kindly saw you on board the vessel for Charleston, and I slew him! Ha, ha, ha! He is no longer a rival of mine."

"Monster! What have I done to thee that you should crush me thus?"

"You preferred Manly to me; you wounded me beyond forgiveness. I swore revenge, and after waiting for it, two long years, I found it! You are now mine, without a rival. and all hell cannot rob me of thee!"

The exulting fiend left me. Oh, that my eyes had been daggers; they would have killed him.

Determined to live no longer in the same city with such a wretch, I contrived that very night to make my escape, leaving all my apparel, except what I and my child had on, and taking my money and jewels (which I had not as yet disposed of,) with my child in my arms, I left the house and took my way towards the city, which I reached about daylight the next morning. I had no difficulty in procuring a passage for Boston, and was soon on board a packet for that port.

[There appeared to be something wanting here, in the MS. It went on:]

My child, I leave you to the care of one who, I fear not will cherish thee as tenderly as I could do were I spared to thee. She has been herself a mother, and that tie that bound her to her offspring, will encircle thee.

Fare thee well,

Thy mother, Cecilia Manly.

It is impossible to do justice to Annie's feelings while reading this account of her parent's sufferings. Her voice was choked and broken by her sobs, and her tears were incessant.

When she had finished reading the manuscript, she felt for her father's picture —it was not to be found! Vainly she searched the ground round about, and felt among the dry leaves; all to no purpose, and almost frantic with her loss, she hastened to the Asylum to acquaint Madame Jerome.

Annie had scarcely disappeared, when the Englishman (whom we have seen about the grounds) left the concealment of a large tree standing near the bench, with the missing picture in his hand. Annie had been so wholly absorbed in her mother's story that he had approached unseen by her, and made himself master of it.

But there was an apparent change in the Englishman's whole appearance.—The habitually cold, harsh expression of his face was no longer visible. He had been deeply moved, and his face bore marks of recent tears. With an unsteady step he gained the bench Annie had just left, and sank upon it.

"Oh, wretch that I was, to doubt such an angel!" he cried. "With two whole years of exemplary life to plead for her—with not a look that should raise a doubt of her truth—not a deed that should raise a blush on the cheek of virtue—her heart laid open to my view, like a garden so richly grown with flowers, it left no room for the weeds of sin to root themselves; and yet, with all this to plead for her—without one ray of evidence against her, but what a fool would have seen was all contrived, I cast her off—my child, too—to go, I cared not whither. Oh dupe! Oh wretch! All the misery I have endured was richly earned; all, all!" —and the miserable man bowed his head upon his breast, and sobbed like a child, in the fulness of his repentant heart.

"And that sweet girl," he continued, "whom I have followed for days, and felt a soothing at my sinking heart when she was near, is my child—my Annie! Oh how I longed to clasp her to my heart, this isolated, aching heart; but shame kept me back. I see her now, as a little child, creeping at my feet, and, pulling herself up, and clinging to my knees till I should take her in my arms, and then nestling on my breast, her rosy lips close to mine, ask a father's kiss! Oh how wel I remember it all! And I remember, too, as if it were but yesterday, the sweet prattle of her little tongue—her shrill, joyous laugh, when in a creeping chase for a grasshopper that found its way in at the open window. Now she nears the tiny object of her desire, her little hand opens to seize the treasure, when lo ! a little spring, and it is beyond her reach. Nothing discouraged, she renews the shout and chase, only to be foiled again ; and so around the room, until the grasshopper, as if tired of the sport, disappears as it came in. How well I remember the lip she made at the sore disappointment. Cecilia pityingly caught her up and nestled her in her bosom, and I laughed—ha, ha, ha !"

Thus carried back to his once happy home, his wife and child about him, the wretched man was for a moment happy.

✻ " But that was more than sixteen years ago," he continued with a sigh, " and I have since travelled hundreds on hundreds of miles, over sea and land—not to seek forgiveness of an injured wife, but with hatred gnawing at my heart, swearing vengeance on her accursed seducer. Oh, I deserve all I have suffered—all !"

The Englishman (whom the reader will have discovered to be Lord Manly) was roused from the violent reproaches on himself, by approaching footsteps ; and divining in his heart that it was his child returning to renew her search for the lost picture, and feeling it impossible to meet her with his present feelings, he hastened to his former place of concealment.

Manly was right in his conjecture. He had scarcely obtained the cover of the tree, when she made her appearance, in company with Madame Jerome.

" Are you sure you put it on the seat, my child ?" inquired the good woman, apparently as much interested in the fate of the picture as Annie herself.

" Quite sure, mother ; and as I live, here it is now. How very strange that I should have overlooked it, when I was so careful to hunt over the ground, all about."

" It was occasioned by your being very much excited, doubtless, my child."

" But tell me, dear mother," continued Annie, gazing on the picture, " you told me you had seen my poor mother ; have you seen my father, too ?"

" Many years ago, my child."

" Does this picture look as he did then ?"

Madame Jerome took the picture, and as her eyes fell full upon it, an attentive observer would have noticed, that though she tried to appear calm, she was deeply moved by thoughts the picture had occasioned.

Manly had come from behind the tree, and stood anxiously watching his daughter and Madame Jerome.

Annie was standing a step behind Madame Jerome, also intent on the picture, but the rustling produced by Manly's movement attracted her attention. Her eyes dwelt for a moment on his face, and then returned to the picture and back again to Manly with the rapidity of thought, and catching Madame Jerome by the arm, she exclaimed,

" It is—it is—"

" Thy father !" shrieked Madame Jerome, and sank fainting on the ground.

Annie rushed into her father's arms.—He folded her to the heart that had so long been childless, kissed her tenderly on the forehead, and then turned his attention to Madame Jerome. Kneeling by her side, he raised her up and rested her head on his breast.

" Pardon, pardon, Cecilia !" he cried passionately. " Let me hear thee speak that forgiving word, and come death willingly. Pardon for doubting virtue like thine ; pardon for all I have caused thee to suffer through long years of exile ; pardon for the misery of this hour—pardon, pardon ! Look up, Cecilia, my wife ! let me hear that voice that used, in sweet keyed tones, to welcome me at morning, noon, or even. Let me look into those eyes again, that used to flash in love to mine, and from their silent yet sparkling depths, let me read my forgiveness."

" Kneel my child," continued Manly to Annie, who stood by trembling with thrilling joy at the new relationship discovered by her father's words. " Kneel my child, and implore forgiveness for thy repentant father. She cannot withstand thy kind entreaties."

Annie knelt, and took her mother's hand affectionately between her own.—
Madame Jerome opened her eyes.

"Mother!" murmured the girl, in that soft, full, tremulous tone known only to
the woman of deep, passionate feelings.

"My daughter!" exclaimed Madame Jerome, straining Annie to her heart,
"you are indeed my daughter."

Manly looked on, his eyes almost blinded with his tears. His wife that had
been lost to him for sixteen years, was restored—his child, too. Oh, how his heart
ached with joy. The husband and wife, father and child, mother and daughter,
were restored to each other ; their hearts so long estranged, were reunited.

   *   *   *   *   *   *   *

One hour after. Let us look in upon the happy family. Lady Manly (for-
merly Madame Jerome) occupied her easy chair. Lord Manly was by her side,
holding the hand of his daughter seated at their feet. By the expression of each
happy face, it was evident that their joy was complete, their hearts running over
with the fulness of content. Annie, in the happiness of her mother, and the joy
of beholding her father, for the moment forgot everything of self and was happy.

Manly was relating to his wife and child what took place after Lady Manly
received his note, not revealed to her by Savile when exulting over the misery he
had wrought.

"The villainy he ascribed to himself," said Manly, "was true, except where my
life was concerned. We fought, and I was wounded, though not dangerously.—
Learning that Savile had followed you to America, though I could not justly complain, after my brutal conduct towards you, I—"

"Do not speak of that. Believing me guilty, as you did, you were justified in
your severity."

"No, Cecilia. I should not have condemned you without a hearing. In that I
sinned. But I must confess, when I learned that Savile had borne you company,
my jealousy knew no bounds, which helped not a little to retard my recovery. In
four weeks I was out, however, and, swearing the most deadly revenge upon Savile,
and feeling little love for you, I followed in the first packet for Charleston. I found
your name on the books at——Hotel, but that gave me no clue to your whereabouts.
The landlord could give me no satisfactory information. I employed men to assist
me in my search, and for two months kept it up unceasingly. But it all proved
fruitless. Despairing, I left for Savannah. There my search was also unavailing, and ever since I have kept it up, from place to place, city to city, and
with such feelings as left but little room for happiness. After sixteen years,
when hope of revenge was almost dead, I met you at the theatre. You recognized
me."

"I did, and fainted. When I came to myself, I was in the open street ; friends
were about me, but no where were you to be seen. I believed it to be an halluci-
nation, and treated it as such. But now, dear Ernest, now that you are indeed
restored to me and our dear Annie, now that you know me innocent of the crime I
should blush to mention, let us forget the past. Blot it out of remembrance, as a
day idly spent ; and for the future consult each other's happiness on the welfare of
our child."

"Noble, generous soul ! How very like you ! But in this I must make some
amends. 'Tis I that have outraged the very name of husband. I have broken
every cord that bound us in happier days. I am no longer thy husband. I have no
claim on thee by the laws of God or man. But if, indeed, the persecutions I have
subjected you to have not changed the love you once bore me into hate,—if you
will again trust your happiness to my keeping, again at the altar will I swear to
keep it sacred. And I will keep my oath, this time, believe me."

"I doubt it not. I would trust then without that oath ; but as you desire it, be
it so."

The door opened, and a servant announced Mr. Erwin.

CHAPTER XVIII.

THE REVENGE.

"How rash, how inconsistent is rage!
How wretched—oh, how fatal is our error,
When to revenge precipitate we run!
Revenge, that still with double force recoils
Back on itself, and is its own revenge."

NIGHT hung over the city, and Cambridge-street was again thronged with its concupiscential crowd, and the doors of the numerous tap-rooms were swung wide, and the different coloured decanters, arranged on shelves, silently invited each passer-by to enter.

It was some minutes past ten o'clock, when a man, habited in a heavy surtout coat and slouched hat, entered the street. He took from a large pocket in the coat a small whip-cord, one end of which was made into a hangman's knot, with the design to see if it was rightly arranged. Finding the noose to play easily on the cord, he replaced it in his pocket, and made his way down the street till he came to the "Rat Trap," when, turning into a dark narrow alley, he disappeared.

In a few minutes he re-appeared upon the street, and entered the tap-room. It had its usual numbers of hangers-on, who gave way as he approached the bar. Turning out a stiff glass of brandy, he quickly swallowed it, and, without a word to any one, went out at the back-door of the tap-room.

"There's a hard customer for you," said a little red-haired, red-faced fellow with a pimply nose.

"He's a black customer," said another.

"Black as the devil," said a third.

"He's a handsome one," observed a prim little girl, with light curling hair, and sparkling eyes.

"What do you know about handsome devils, I should like to know?" growled the red-faced gentleman who spoke first.

"Very little till I cut your company," retorted the girl.

At this there was a laugh raised at the red-faced gentleman's expense; he pulled down the corners of his mouth, and was—mum.

"Who is he?" asked Mr. Thirdly, of the man in waiting behind the bar.

"That's more than I can tell. I've been told he was deuced rich, but I've a notion that old Ned's got the largest piece by this time, for he comes here oftener than is healthy for him."

While these remarks were being made in the tap-room, the object of them had made his way into old Ned's apartments. The old man, as usual, was brooding over a grate (half filled) of smouldering Newcastle coal.

"Are you alone, Mr. Barnabee?" asked Freelove, in a voice unusually harsh and discordant.

The old man rose at the voice.

"Ah, is it you, Mr. Freelove? Still with that disguise on, I see. What can I do to serve you?"

"Are we alone?"

"We are; but why this secrecy? Have you another cheque you want cashed?"

"Not at present; but I have something to communicate that deeply concerns us both. Will you step into the next room?"

"No one will intrude upon us here, Mr. Freelove."

"Perhaps not; but I shall be better pleased if you will take the next room for our conference. The very important nature of my communication makes me doubly mistrustful."

"We are so far from the tap-room, that we shall not be disturbed from that quarter; and I have no prying bodies about me, Mr. Freelove," said Barnabee, with a knowing wink.

"I am glad to hear it."

"I have an eye singly to my fair reputat'on, Mr. Freelove; but, to make you feel more at home, we will take the next room."

Barnabee took the lamp, and led the way.

"This room is not so cheerful as the one we have left, Mr. Freelove. I keep no fire in this—coal is so dear."

"It matters little to me," said Freelove, significantly, closing and locking the door.

"Why do you lock the door, Mr. Freelove? Did I not say we should not be intruded upon?"

"I like to satisfy myself, sir."

If Barnabee had seen the expression of Freelove's face, all this time—had seen the iron hardness of his visage—had marked the veins in his forehead swollen almost to bursting—his teeth set firmly together; he would have been less courtly in his bearing towards him.

While old Ned was arranging two chairs for their accommodation, quick as thought Freelove had the rope we have before seen in his possession, over his head, and the other end thrown over a hook in the ceiling, once used to suspend a hanging lamp, and the old man drawn up to his full height, by the neck.

So sudden was this movement—so entirely was Barnabee taken by surprise, that he did not cry out, but stood on his toes' ends, to keep him from being choked outright.

"He, he, ha, ha, ha!" laughed Barnabee, in a voice intended to be mirthful, but which, nevertheless, savoured more of the quakings of fear than pleasantry; getting his fingers between the rope and his neck. "This is a delightful joke! he, he, he, capital joke, Mr. Freelove. But be so kind as not to pull the rope quite so taut—ease away a little, so I can bear my weight upon my feet."

"Truly a capital joke—worthy my invention! How do you relish your present position, Mr. Barnabee?" said Freelove, tauntingly, looking at the old man, (who with all his pretending to treat the matter as a joke, was almost dead with fright,) with a sort of fiendish satisfaction.

"Can't say I relish it very much; no doubt it has less charms for me than for you, Mr. Freelove, and if you will slack up the rope, I shall take it as a personal favour, as my toes begin to feel tired."

"Look you old man," said Freelove, severely, "you may treat this matter as lightly as you will, but before you get through with it, you will learn, that some things can be done as well as others."

"I don't feel disposed to dispute it, Mr. Freelove. Having yielded this point, you will be so good as to yield on your part."

"Listen, old man! for more than six months you have had me by the neck. You would not let me breathe unless I gave you two dollars for every one you were pleased to advance me. You have been honey and vinegar by turns. When there was any prospect of making money out of me, you have fawned around me and called me Mr., and Your honour, and dog-like licked my very feet! But when you have had me at your mercy you have spit upon me. The table has turned now, old man. I now have you by the neck, and in my hatred, and the damning wrongs you have done me, I'll not relax my hold till the breath is out of your villainous body. If I allow you to breathe now, it is that you may hear me, and for a moment look on death before you take the final leap."

Barnabee, now more than ever convinced, that it was no boy's play, made an effort to an alarm; but he was instantly drawn off his feet, and his voice died away into a low gurgling sound in his throat.

"Try to alarm the house, and that moment is your last!" cried Freelove, in a terrible voice, at the same time letting Barnabee back upon his feet. "I would not kill you yet, for you have not heard me out."

"You cannot be serious, Mr. Freelove?"

"Look in my face—do you see anything that bids you hope? Now look at the door. It is fastened ; and before any one could come to your assistance, you would be beyond his mercy ; and if you can turn your head, you will see that the window-shutters are secured from without; you see I had prepared myself for it before-hand."

"What do you want with me?" cried the miserable old man, more dead than alive.

"What I will have, thy life."

"It will do you no good."

"I shall have revenge for the life you have taken from me."

"I have not taken your life."

"Innocent, indeed! But you have taken from me all that makes life desirable, my patrimony."

"Give me back the money I have loaned you, and I will give you back all I have of yours."

"Marvellous, marvellous! I did not think you could be brought to do that—I have misjudged you! But see you not, when I have made a finish of you, I can help myself from your strong box?"

"Would you rob me!" shrieked the old man, making another attempt to free himself ; but he was seasonably warned that such another attempt would prove dangerous, and was silent.

"No," said Freelove, "I will not rob you; I will only take what you have robbed me of. By searching the records, I find the instrument making over to you my estate has not been recorded ; I have only to destroy that, and the estate is mine again."

Barnabee groaned aloud.

"So much for the wrongs you have done me," continued Freelove. "And now for my sister's wrongs. Ha, ha! does thy conscience tell thee what is coming Villain! how canst thou hope to live after this?"

With the last words, Freelove began to haul upon the rope.

"Mercy, mercy!" cried the miserable old man, his knees knocking together with mortal fear.

"Mercy, old man! What is thy miserable life that I should spare it, after the evil you have done me and mine? Quick, make my sister all the reparation in thy power—provide for her child ; and then make thy peace with God, and then die!"

"Her child!"

"Ay, thy child, wretch! Give thy gold for its support, and give unsparingly too ; for I rather it should be a gift, than that I should take it from thee. My conscience would be easier, I trow. Quick, for time passes! What do you say?"

"Spare my life, and I will give up all I have taken from you, freely and un-conditionally."

For a moment Freelove seemed to waver. The old man saw it, and jumped at it, as a drowing man at a straw. Death no longer stared him in the face! he should live! A few more years would be left to him, to plot, to scheme, and get rich.

"The gift I will accept," at length said Freelove, and then seeing Barnabee's face brighten he continued, " but do not hope to escape me! The wrongs you have done cannot be atoned for with gold. The misery and disgrace you have brought upon our family, call for vengeance——"

"'Vengeance is mine, saith the Lord!'"

"Such language coming from thee, is blasphemy, old man! But I would gladly wash my hands of your false blood. If I accept your offer and spare your life, what surety have I that you will not make this night's transactions public?"

"By my hopes of salvation, I will not."

"The chance is small, but I will trust you, believing for your own sake you will keep silent. Give me the papers."

"With this rope around my neck?"

"Ay, with a rope around your neck! I know better than to trust you; you get not your head out of the jaws of death until I have the papers safely in my own hands. I will slacken the rope so that you can reach your drawers; but mark me, sir; if you try to slip your neck out you will have the satisfaction of another choaking."

The rope was slackened, and the old man tremblingly approached a case of drawers, and took from them the paper by which he held Freelove's property, and placed it in his hand,

Freelove then took the rope from Barnabee's neck, who, now that the excitement and danger were past, no longer able to bear up under the sufferings he had gone through, sank upon the floor.

And so Freelove left him.

CHAPTER XIX.

THE GOLDEN MARRIAGE.

"Bride and bridegroom, pilgrims of life, henceforward to travel together,
In this the beginning of your journey, neglect not the favour of Heaven;
And at eventide kneel ye together, that your joys be not unhallowed.
Angels that are round you shall be glad, those loving ministers of mercy,
And the richest blessings of your God shall be poured on his favoured children."

SCENE FIRST.

THREE months had passed away, and all was again astir among the little ones of St. Mary. The little girls were attired in their holiday dresses, and favours were worn by the servants, according to the good old English style. The morning was bright and promising, and the lawn was being pressed with the tiny foot of many a light-hearted girl.

"What upon arth be yer gwoin to du with that hoop of posies?" asked Seth of a pretty miss, who, with others, was leaving the garden—she with a garland of roses, the others with bouquets of different flowers.

"It is a coronet I have prepared for Annie's brow," she answered.

"I rather calkerlate you're glad she's gwoin' away, ain't ye?"

"Not I indeed. She is the sweetest young lady I ever knew."

"I see nothing very sweet about her," said another girl of about the same age.

"O you git out, now! you're as jealous as rotten pizen, 'cause you think she is handsomer nor you."

"I have much to do, I should think, to be jealous of her."

"You're as jealous as all; git out, now; that's jest as clear as preachin'. You haint got no posies for her; that's the most pertikilar kind of sartenty you're jealous. You'd better look out, or you'll turn yaller with it, sarten as you're live."

The girl pouted, and left the garden.

"That gal's lavin' a nest-egg for a hull lot of misery. You'd better go and take care of the new babby," he continued, crying after the girl leaving the garden; and then, turning to the girl with the wreath, he said, "Have you seen the little human critter?"

"I found it on the door stone this morning, when I'se gwoin' out. I tuk the cloth off purty mighty quick, and lo and behold it was only a little human babby, fast asleep, arter all."

"Is what you tell me true?"

"True! Just cum and take a look at the little critter."

SCENE SECOND.

It was three months since Annie had found her parents, and she sat alone, in a private room of St. Mary. She was happy, and yet tears stood in her eyes. She was reading a letter.

Erwin entered the room.

"Tears on our wedding-day, dearest?" he said affectionately.

"But tears of joy, Philip, for I have just heard from a dear friend, whose happiness next to yours and my dear parents', I most fervently pray for. You have heard me speak of Charles?"

"I have."

"Here is a letter written from him. Sit down—you shall hear it."

"Nay, dearest; it is not intended for my ears."

"Anything you should not hear, I should blush at receiving."

"My own true Annie!"

SCENE THIRD.

A procession of little girls and maidens, two by two, were entering the chapel. They were all dressed alike, and each wore a rose in her bosom, with the exception of the girl whom Seth accused of jealousy. She wore none, and her face looked less happy than those of her companions. That she wore no rose in her bosom, was unnoticed, perhaps, by all, if we except Seth. He observed it, and remarked, with more feeling than he usually evinced,—

"I hope she aint got no thorn there instid, any how."

Then followed Lord Manly and Lady Manly, and after them Annie and Erwin. They approached the altar, where stood the priest in his sacred robes. How glowed Annie's cheek—how trembled her little hand, when she placed it in the hand of him she was about to call her husband! He too, gazing upon his young and handsome bride, looked proud and happy.

SCENE FOURTH.

Helen was reclining on a sofa, and her pale and sinking features were almost painful to behold. Her brother sat at the window, gloomy and abstracted. At length Helen spoke.

"I have been thinking brother," she said in a faint voice, "that we had better leave the city."

"Where shall we go?" he asked despondingly.

"Anywhere you choose, brother. You have lost all relish for society here; you scarcely go out the whole day."

"Say rather that society is lost to me. How can I go out? They point at me as I walk along, and say, 'There goes Tom Freelove; his sister is—'"

"Do not reproach me now; or if you will, reproach on; I shall not be here to bear it, and for your sake I wish I might die now. We can go into the country, brother; its quietness will be soothing to our tried spirits."

"Humph! Think you not our disgrace will follow us there?"

"Go not thither then. At least we can go to New York, without fear of being known."

"I doubt if we can do that."

"Is there any one there you are acquainted with?"

"Yes, that boorish clown, Snooksby.—He starved it here till starving wouldn't do any good, and then he diddled the packet master out of the passage money to New York, where he has made himself quite a lion."

"We can change our names, brother, and in that large city I do not fear he will discover us. And with our present wealth you can live as gaily as you please. For myself, I only wish for a place where I can live undisturbed, and forgotten, die."

"Have it your own way, I only wish to go where I can hold up my head again, and be what I have been."

The door opened, and Mary entered the room. Helen sprung to meet her, but sank back again exhausted on the sofa.

"Well, Mary, what have you done with it?" she exclaimed eagerly, though faintly.

"I got there just before daylight, marm, and left the basket on the front door steps. I then went back into the grove, where I could watch and see if it was taken care of."

"Bless you! bless you!"

"In about an hour, the door opened, and a man came out. He seemed much surprised at seeing the basket, but after a minute he took off the cloth and carried it into the Asylum."

"I shall never see my child again," cried the unhappy Helen, "never! never!" and she buried her face in the pillow of the sofa, and wept the last sad tears of her isolated, broken heart.

Mary tried every argument to comfort her, and succeeded at last in drying her tears.

"They are making preparations for Erwin's marriage with Madame Jerome's newly-acknowledged daughter," said Freelove angrily. "And the old lady is to be re-married, as I hear, to a runaway husband of sixteen years' separation. Success to them, say I."

Helen took no notice of her brother's angry expressions, but desired Mary to fetch her work-box from the table, and taking from it a well filled purse, she placed it in Mary's hand.

"I regret it, Mary," she said, "but we must part with you. In that purse you will find a sum of money; it is not large, but it is all I have at present to spare, —Take it, it is yours."

"In what have I offended?" asked the girl, tremblingly.

"You have not offended me, Mary.—On the contrary, you have been kind, and have always served me faithfully, I am going to leave the city; you of course will not like to follow me."

Mary's face brightened, and putting the purse back into Helen's hand, she said,—

"I will never leave you marm unless you send me away."

Helen was moved by this show of affection from one she had no right to expect it from. She made no answer, nor thanked the girl, but with her looks.

*   *   *   *   *   *   *   *   *   *

Erwin and Annie were blessed in their happy union, and in their after life reaped the goodly seed sown in their youth. Blessed in themselves, and in the little ones lent them for their support in old age, they lived doing good, and happy.